Melod

The Story of a

Laura Elizabeth Howe Richards

Alpha Editions

This edition published in 2022

ISBN : 9789356894778

Design and Setting By
Alpha Editions
www.alphaedis.com
Email - info@alphaedis.com

Contents

CHAPTER I.

THE CHILD.

"Well, there!" said Miss Vesta. "The child has a wonderful gift, that is certain. Just listen to her, Rejoice! You never heard our canary sing like that!"

Miss Vesta put back the shutters as she spoke, and let a flood of light into the room where Miss Rejoice lay. The window was open, and Melody's voice came in like a wave of sound, filling the room with sweetness and life and joy.

"It's like the foreign birds they tell about!" said Miss Rejoice, folding her thin hands, and settling herself on the pillow with an air of perfect content,— "nightingales, and skylarks, and all the birds in the poetry-books. What is she doing, Vesta?"

Miss Rejoice could see part of the yard from her bed. She could see the white lilac-bush, now a mass of snowy plumes, waving in the June breeze; she could see the road, and knew when any of the neighbors went to town or to meeting; but the corner from which the wonderful voice came thrilling and soaring was hidden from her.

Miss Vesta peered out between the muslin curtains. "She's sitting on the steps," she said, "feeding the hens. It is wonderful, the way the creatures know her! That old top-knot hen, that never has a good word for anybody, is sitting in her lap almost. She says she understands their talk, and I really believe she does. 'Tis certain none of them cluck, not a sound, while she's singing. 'Tis a manner of marvel, to my mind."

"It is so," assented Miss Rejoice, mildly. "There, sister! you said you had never heard her sing 'Tara's Harp.' Do listen now!"

Both sisters were silent in delight. Miss Vesta stood at the window, leaning against the frame. She was tall, and straight as an arrow, though she was fifty years old. Her snow-white hair was brushed straight up from her broad forehead; her blue eyes were keen and bright as a sword. She wore a black dress and a white apron; her hands showed the marks of years of serving, and of hard work of all kinds. No one would have thought that she and Miss Rejoice were sisters, unless he had surprised one of the loving looks that sometimes passed between them when they were alone together. The face that lay on the pillow was white and withered, like a crumpled white rose. The dark eyes had a pleading, wistful look, and were wonderfully soft withal. Miss Rejoice had white hair too, but it had a warm yellowish tinge, very different from the clear white of Miss Vesta's. It curled, too, in little ringlets round her beautiful old face. In short, Miss Vesta was splendidly handsome, while no one would think of calling Miss Rejoice anything but lovely. The younger sister lay always in bed. It was some thirty years since she met with the accident which changed her from a rosy, laughing girl into a helpless cripple. A party of pleasure,—gay lads and lasses riding together, careless of anything save the delight of the moment; a sudden leap of the horse, frightened at some obstacle; a fall, striking on a sharp stone,—this was Miss Rejoice's little story. People in the village had forgotten that there was any story; even her own contemporaries almost forgot that Rejoice had ever been other than she was now. But Miss Vesta never forgot. She left her position in the neighboring town, broke off her engagement to the man she loved, and came home to her sister; and they had never been separated for a day since. Once, when the bitter pain began to abate, and the sufferer could realize that she was still a living creature and not a condemned spirit, suffering for the sins of some one else (she had thought of all her own, and could not feel that they were bad enough to merit such suffering, if God was the person she supposed),—in those first days Miss Rejoice ventured to question her sister about her engagement. She was afraid—she did hope the breaking of it had nothing to do with her. "It has to do with myself!" said Miss Vesta, briefly, and nothing more was said. The sisters had lived their life together, without a thought save for each other, till Melody came into their world.

But here is Melody at the door; she shall introduce herself. A girl of twelve years old, with a face like a flower. A broad white forehead, with dark hair curling round it in rings and tendrils as delicate as those of a vine; a sweet, steadfast mouth, large blue eyes, clear and calm under the long dark lashes, but with a something in them which makes the stranger turn to look at them again. He may look several times before he discovers the reason of their fixed, unchanging calm. The lovely mouth smiles, the exquisite face lights up with gladness or softens into sympathy or pity; but the blue eyes do not flash or soften, for Melody is blind.

She came into the room, walking lightly, with a firm, assured tread, which gave no hint of hesitation or uncertainty.

"See, Aunt Joy," she said brightly, "here is the first rose. You were saying yesterday that it was time for cinnamon-roses; now here is one for you." She stooped to kiss the sweet white face, and laid the glowing blossom beside it.

"Thank you, dear," said Miss Rejoice; "I might have known you would find the first blossom, wherever it was. Where was this, now? On the old bush behind the barn?"

"Not in our yard at all," replied the child, laughing. "The smell came to me a few minutes ago, and I went hunting for it. It was in Mrs. Penny's yard, right down by the fence, close, so you could hardly see it."

"Well, I never!" exclaimed Miss Vesta. "And she let you have it?"

"Of course," said the child. "I told her it was for Aunt Joy."

"H'm!" said Miss Vesta. "Martha Penny doesn't suffer much from giving, as a rule, to Aunt Joy or anybody else. Did she give it to you at the first asking, hey?"

"Now, Vesta!" remonstrated Miss Rejoice, gently.

"Well, I want to know," persisted the elder sister.

Melody laughed softly. "Not quite the first asking," she said. "She wanted to know if I thought she had no nose of her own. 'I didn't mean that,' said I; 'but I thought perhaps you wouldn't care for it quite as much as Aunt Joy would.' And when she asked why, I said, 'You don't sound as if you would.' Was that rude, Aunt Vesta?"

"Humph!" said Miss Vesta, smiling grimly. "I don't know whether it was exactly polite, but Martha Penny wouldn't know the difference."

The child looked distressed, and so did Miss Rejoice.

"I am sorry," said Melody. "But then Mrs. Penny said something so funny. 'Well, gaffle onto it! I s'pose you're one of them kind as must always have what they want in this world. Gaffle onto your rose, and go 'long! Guess I might be sick enough before anybody 'ud get roses for me!' So I told her I would bring her a whole bunch of our white ones as soon as they were out, and told her how I always tried to get the first cinnamon-rose for Aunt Joy. She said, 'She ain't your aunt, nor mine either.' But she spoke kinder, and didn't seem cross any more; so I took the rose, and here it is."

Miss Vesta was angry. A bright spot burned in her cheeks, and she was about to speak hastily; but Miss Rejoice raised a gentle hand, and motioned her to be silent.

"Martha Penny has a sharp way, Melody," said Miss Rejoice; "but she meant no unkindness, I think. The rose is very sweet," she added; "there are no other roses so sweet, to my mind. And how are the hens this morning, dearie?"

The child clapped her hands, and laughed aloud. "Oh, we have had such fun!" she cried. "Top-knot was very cross at first, and would not let the young speckled hen eat out of the dish with her. So I took one under each arm, and sang and talked to them till they were both in a good humor. That made the Plymouth rooster jealous, and he came and drove them both away, and had to have a petting all by himself. He is such a dear!"

"You do spoil those hens, Melody," said Miss Vesta, with an affectionate grumble. "Do you suppose they'll eat any better for being talked to and sung to as if they were persons?"

"Poor dears!" said the child; "they ought to be happy while they do live, oughtn't they, Auntie? Is it time to make the cake now, Aunt Vesta, or shall I get my knitting, and sing to Auntie Joy a little?"

At that moment a clear whistle was heard outside the house. "The doctor!" cried Melody, her sightless face lighting up with a flash of joy. "I must go," and she ran quickly out to the gate.

"Now he'll carry her off," said Miss Vesta, "and we sha'n't see her again till dinner-time. You'd think she was his child, not ours. But so it is, in this world."

"What has crossed you this morning, Sister?" asked Miss Rejoice, mildly. "You seem put about."

"Oh, the cat got into the tea-kettle." replied the elder sister. "Don't fret your blessed self if I am cross. I can't stand Martha Penny, that's all,—speaking so to that blessed child! I wish I had her here; she'd soon find out whether she had a nose or not. Dear knows it's long enough! It isn't the first time I've had four parts of a mind to pull it for her."

"Why, Vesta Dale, how you do talk!" said Miss Rejoice, and then they both laughed, and Miss Vesta went out to scold the doctor.

CHAPTER II.

THE DOCTOR.

The doctor sat in his buggy, leaning forward, and talking to the child. A florid, jovial-looking man, bright-eyed and deep-chested, with a voice like a trumpet, and a general air of being the West Wind in person. He was not alone this time: another doctor sat beside him; and Miss Vesta smoothed her ruffled front at sight of the stranger.

"Good-morning, Vesta," shouted the doctor, cheerily. "You came out to shoot me, because you thought I was coming to carry off Melody, eh? You needn't say no, for I know your musket-shot expression. Dr. Anthony, let me present you to Miss Vesta Dale,—a woman who has never had the grace to have a day's sickness since I have known her, and that's forty years at least."

"Miss Dale is a fortunate woman," said Dr. Anthony, smiling. "Have you many such constitutions in your practice, Brown?"

"I am fool enough to wish I had," growled Dr Brown. "That woman, sir, is enough to ruin any practice, with her pernicious example of disgusting health. How is Rejoice this morning, Vesta? Does she want to see me?"

Miss Vesta thought not, to-day; then followed questions and answers, searching on one side, careful and exact on the other; and then—

"I should like it if you could spare Melody for half an hour this morning," said the doctor. "I want her to go down to Phoebe Jackson's to see little Ned."

"Oh, what is the matter with Ned?" cried Melody, with a quick look of alarm.

"Tomfoolery is the principal matter with him, my dear," said Dr. Brown, grimly. "His eyes have been troubling him, you know, ever since he had the measles in the winter. I've kept one eye on the child, knowing that his mother was a perfect idiot, or rather, an imperfect one, which is worse. Yesterday she sent for me in hot haste: Ned was going blind, and would I please come that minute, and save the precious child, and oh, dear me, what should she do, and all the rest of it. I went down mad enough, I can tell you; found the child's eyes looking like a ploughed field. 'What have you been doing to this child, Phffibe?' 'We-ell, Doctor, his eyes has been kind o' bad along back, the last week. I did cal'late to send for you before; but one o' the neighbors was in, and she said to put molasses and tobacco-juice in them.' 'Thunder and turf!' says I. 'What sa-ay?' says Phoebe. "N' then old Mis' Barker come in last night. You know she's had consid'able experi'nce with eyes, her own having been weakly, and all her children's after her. And *she* said to try vitriol; but I kind o' thought I'd ask you first, Doctor, so I waited till morning. And now his eyes look terrible, and he seems dretful 'pindlin'; oh, dear me, what shall I do if my poor little Neddy goes blind?' 'Do, Madam?' I said. 'You will have the satisfaction of knowing that you and your tobacco-juice and molasses have made him blind. That's what you will do, and much good may it do you.'"

"Oh, Doctor," cried Melody, shrinking as if the words had been addressed to her, "how could you say that? But you don't think—you don't think Ned will really be blind?" The child had grown very pale, and she leaned over the gate with clasped hands, in painful suspense.

"No, I don't," replied the doctor. "I think he will come out all right; no thanks to his mother if he does. But it was necessary to frighten the woman, Melody, for fright is the only thing that makes an impression on a fool. Now, I want you to run down there, like a good child; that is, if your aunts can spare you. Run down and comfort the little fellow, who has been badly scared by the clack of tongues and the smarting of the tobacco-juice. Imbeciles! cods' heads! scooped-out pumpkins!" exclaimed the doctor, in a sudden frenzy. "A—I don't mean that. Comfort him up, child, and sing to him and tell him about Jack-and-the-Beanstalk. You'll soon bring him round, I'll warrant. But stop," he added, as the child, after touching Miss Vesta's hand lightly, and making and receiving I know not what silent communication, turned toward the house,—"stop a moment, Melody. My friend Dr. Anthony here is very fond of music, and he would like to hear you sing just one song. Are you in singing trim this morning?"

The child laughed. "I can always sing, of course," she said simply. "What song would you like, Doctor?"

"Oh, the best," said Dr. Brown. "Give us 'Annie Laurie.'"

The child sat down on a great stone that stood beside the gate. It was just under the white lilac-bush, and the white clusters bent lovingly down over her, and seemed to murmur with pleasure as the wind swept them lightly to and fro. Miss Vesta said something about her bread, and gave an uneasy glance toward the house, but she did not go in; the window was open, and Rejoice could hear; and after all, bread was not worth so much as "Annie Laurie." Melody folded her hands lightly on her lap, and sang.

Dr. Brown thought "Annie Laurie" the most beautiful song in the world; certainly it is one of the best beloved. Ever since it was first written and sung (who knows just when that was? "Anonymous" is the legend that stands in the song-books beside this familiar title. We do not know the man's name, cannot visit the place where he wrote and sang, and made music for all coming generations of English-speaking people; can only think of him as a kind friend, a man of heart and genius as surely as if his name stood at the head of unnumbered symphonies and fugues),—ever since it was first sung, I say, men and women and children have loved this song. We hear of its being sung by camp-fires, on ships at sea, at gay parties of pleasure. Was it not at the siege of Lucknow that it floated like a breath from home through the city hell-beset, and brought cheer and hope and comfort to all who heard it? The cotter's wife croons it over her sleeping baby; the lover sings it to his sweetheart; the child runs, carolling it, through the summer fields; finally, some world-honored prima-donna, some Patti or Nilsson, sings it as the final touch of perfection to a great feast of music, and hearts swell and eyes overflow to find that the nursery song of our childhood is a world-song, immortal in freshness and beauty. But I am apt to think that no lover, no tender mother, no splendid Italian or noble Swede, could sing "Annie Laurie" as Melody sang it. Sitting there in her simple cotton dress, her head thrown slightly back, her hands folded, her eyes fixed in their unchanging calm, she made a picture that the stranger never forgot. He started as the first notes of her voice stole forth, and hung quivering on the air,—

"Maxwellton braes are bonnie,
Where early fa's the dew."

What wonder was this? Dr. Anthony had come prepared to hear, he quite knew what,—a child's voice, pretty, perhaps, thin and reedy, nasal, of course. His good friend Brown was an excellent physician, but with no knowledge of music; how should he have any, living buried in the country, twenty miles from a railway, forty miles from a concert? Brown had said so much about the blind child that it would have been discourteous for him, Dr. Anthony, to refuse to see and hear her when he came to pass a night with his old college chum; but his assent had been rather wearily given: Dr. Anthony detested juvenile prodigies. But what was this? A voice full and round as the voices of Italy; clear as a bird's; swelling ever richer, fuller, rising in tones so pure, so noble, that the heart of the listener ached, as the poet's heart at hearing the nightingale, with almost painful pleasure. Amazement and delight made Dr. Anthony's face a study, which his friend perused with keen enjoyment. He knew, good Dr. Brown, that he himself was a musical nobody; he knew pretty well (what does a doctor not know?) what Anthony was thinking as they drove along. But he knew Melody too; and he rubbed his hands, and chuckled inwardly at the discomfiture of his knowing friend.

The song died away; and the last notes were like those of the skylark when she sinks into her nest at sunset. The listeners drew breath, and looked at each other.

There was a brief silence, and then, "Thank you, Melody," said Dr. Brown. "That's the finest song in the world, I don't care what the next is. Now run along, like my good maid, and sing it to Neddy Jackson, and he will forget all about his eyes, and turn into a great pair of ears."

The child laughed. "Neddy will want 'The British Grenadier,'" she said. "That is *his* greatest song." She ran into the house to kiss Miss Rejoice, came out with her sun-bonnet tied under her chin, and lifted her face to kiss Miss Vesta. "I sha'n't be gone long, Auntie," she said brightly. "There'll be plenty of time to make the cake after dinner."

Miss Vesta smoothed the dark hair with a motherly touch. "Doctor doesn't care anything about our cake," she said; "he isn't coming to tea to-night. I suppose you'd better stay as long as you're needed. I should not want the child to fret."

"Good-by, Doctor," cried the child, joyously, turning her bright face toward the buggy. "Good-by, sir," making a little courtesy to Dr. Anthony, who gravely took off his hat and bowed as if to a duchess. "Good-by again, dear auntie;" and singing softly to herself, she walked quickly away.

Dr. Anthony looked after her, silent for a while. "Blind from birth?" he asked presently.

"From birth," replied Dr. Brown. "No hope; I've had Strong down to see her. But she's the happiest creature in the world, I do believe. How does she sing?" he asked with ill-concealed triumph. "Pretty well for a country child, eh?"

"She sings like an angel," said Dr. Anthony,—"like an angel from heaven."

"She has a right to, sir," said Miss Vesta, gravely. "She is a child of God, who has never forgotten her Father."

Dr. Anthony turned toward the speaker, whom he had almost forgotten in his intense interest in the child. "This lovely child is your own niece, Madam?" he inquired. "She must be unspeakably dear to you."

Miss Vesta flushed. She did not often speak as she had just done, being a New England woman; but "Annie Laurie" always carried her out of herself, she declared. The answer to the gentleman's question was one she never liked to make. "She is not my niece in blood," she said slowly. "We are single women, my sister and I; but she is like our own daughter to us."

"Twelve years this very month, Vesta, isn't it," said Dr. Brown, kindly, "since the little one came to you? Do you remember what a wild night it was?"

Miss Vesta nodded. "I hear the wind now when I think of it," she said.

"The child is an orphan," the doctor continued, turning to his friend. "Her mother was a young Irish woman, who came here looking for work.

She was poor, her husband dead, consumption on her, and so on, and so on. She died at the poorhouse, and left this blind baby. Tell Dr. Anthony how it happened, Vesta."

Miss Vesta frowned and blushed. She wished Doctor would remember that his friend was a stranger to her. But in a moment she raised her head. "There's nothing to be ashamed of, after all," she said, a little proudly. "I don't know why I should not tell you, sir. I went up to the poor-farm one evening, to carry a basket of strawberries. We had a great quantity, and I thought some of the people up there might like them, for they had few luxuries, though I don't believe they ever went hungry. And when I came there, Mrs. Green, who kept the farm then, came out looking all in a maze. 'Did you ever hear of such a thing in your life?' she cried out, the minute she set eyes on me. 'I don't know, I'm sure,' said I. 'Perhaps I did, and perhaps I didn't. How's the baby that poor soul left?' I said. It was two weeks since the mother died; and to tell the truth, I went up about as much to see how the child was getting on as to take the strawberries, though I don't know that I realized it till this very minute." She smiled grimly, and went on. "'That's just it,' Mrs. Green screams out, right in my face. 'Dr. Brown has just been here, and he says the child is blind, and will be blind all her days, and we've got to bring her up; and I'd like to know if I haven't got enough to do without feedin' blind children?' I just looked at her. 'I don't know that a deaf woman would be much better than a blind child,' said I; 'so I'll thank you to speak like a human being, Liza Green, and not scream at me. Aren't you ashamed?' I said. 'The child can't help being blind, I suppose. Poor little lamb! as if it hadn't enough, with no father nor mother in the world.' 'I don't care,' says Liza, crazy as ever; 'I can't stand it. I've got all I can stand now, with a feeble-minded boy and two so old they can't feed themselves. That Polly is as crazy as a loon, and the rest is so shif'less it loosens all my j'ints to look at 'em. I won't stand no more, for Dr. Brown nor anybody else.' And she set her hands on her hips and stared at me as if she'd like to eat me, sun-bonnet and all. 'Let me see the child,' I said. I went in, and there it lay,—the prettiest creature you ever saw in your life, with its eyes wide open, just as they are now, and the sweetest look on its little face. Well, there, you'd know it came straight from heaven, if you saw it in—Well, I don't know exactly what I'm saying. You must excuse me, sir!" and Miss Vesta paused in some confusion. "'Somebody ought to adopt it,' said I. 'It's a beautiful child; any one might be proud of it when it grew up.' 'I guess when you find anybody that would adopt a blind child, you'll find the cat settin' on hen's eggs,' said Liza Green. I sat and held the child a little while, trying to think of some one who would be likely to take care of it; but I couldn't think of any one, for as she said, so it was. By and by I kissed the poor little pretty thing, and laid it back in its cradle, and tucked it up well, though it was a warm night. 'You'll take care of that child, Liza,' I said, 'as long as it stays with you, or I'll know the reason why. There are plenty of people who would like the work here, if you're tired of it,' I said. She quieted down at that, for she knew that a word from me would set the doctor to thinking, and he wasn't going to have that blind child slighted, well I knew. Well, sir, I came home, and told Rejoice."

"Her sister," put in Dr. Brown,—"a crippled saint, been in her bed thirty years. She and Melody keep a small private heaven, and Vesta is the only sinner admitted."

"Doctor, you're very profane," said Miss Vesta, reprovingly. "I've never seen my sister Rejoice angry, sir, except that one time, when I told her. 'Where is the child?' she says. 'Why, where do you suppose?' said I. 'In its cradle, of course. I tucked it up well before I came away, and she won't dare to mistreat it for one while,' I said. 'Go and get it!' says my sister Rejoice. 'How dared you come home without it? Go and get it this minute, do you hear?' I stared as if I had seen a vision. 'Rejoice, what are you thinking of?' I asked. 'Bring that child here? Why, what should we do with it? I can't take care of it, nor you either.' My sister turned the color of fire. 'No one else shall take care of it,' she says, as if she was Bunker Hill Monument on a pillow. 'Go and get it this minute, Vesta. Don't wait; the Lord must not be kept waiting. Go, I tell you!' She looked so wild I was fairly frightened; so I tried to quiet her. I thought her mind was touched, some way. 'Well, I'll go to-morrow,' says I, soothing her; 'I couldn't go now, anyhow, Rejoice. Just hear it rain and blow! It came on just as I stepped inside the door, and it's a regular storm now. Be quiet,' I said, 'and I'll go up in the morning and see about it.' My sister sat right up in the bed. 'You'll go now,' she says, 'or I'll go myself. Now, this living minute! Quick!' I went, sir. The fire in her eyes would have scorched me if I had looked at it a minute longer. I thought she was coming out of the bed after me,—she, who had not stirred for twenty years. I caught up a shawl, threw another over my shoulders, and ran for the poor-farm. 'T was a perfect tempest, but I never felt it. Something seemed to drive me, as if it was a whip laid across my shoulders. I thought it was my sister's eyes, that had never looked hard at me since she was born; but maybe it was something else besides. They say there are no miracles in these days, but we don't know everything yet. I ran in at the farm, before them all, dripping, looking like a maniac, I don't doubt. I caught up the child out of the cradle, and wrapped it in the shawl I'd brought, and ran off again before they'd got their eyes shut from staring at me as if I was a spirit of evil. How my breath held out, don't ask me; but I got home, and ran into the chamber, and laid the child down by the side of my sister Rejoice."

Miss Vesta paused, and the shadow of a great awe crept into her keen blue eyes. "The poor-farm was struck by lightning that night!" she said. "The cradle where that baby was lying was shattered into kindling-wood, and Liza Green has never been the same woman from that day to this."

CHAPTER III.

ON THE ROAD.

Melody went singing down the road. She walked quickly, with a light swaying motion, graceful as a bird. Her hands were held before her, not, it seemed, from timidity, but rather as a butterfly stretches out its delicate antennae, touching, feeling, trying its way, as it goes from flower to flower. Truly, the child's light fingers were like butterflies, as she walked beside the road, reaching up to touch the hanging sprays of its bordering willows, or caressing the tiny flowers that sprang up along the footpath. She sang, too, as she went, a song the doctor had taught her:—

"Who is Silvia, and what is she,
That all our swains commend her?
Holy, fair, and wise is she;
The heavens such grace did lend her,
That adored she might be."

One might have thought that Silvia was not far to seek, on looking into the fair face of the child. Now she stopped, and stood for a moment with head thrown back, and nostrils slightly distended. "Meadow-sweet!" she said softly to herself. "Isn't it out early? the dear. I must find it for Aunt Joy." She stooped, and passed her light, quick hands over the wayside grasses. Every blade and leaf was a familiar friend, and she greeted them as she touched them, weaving their names into her song in childish fashion,—

"Buttercup and daisy dear, sorrel for her eating,
Mint and rose to please the nose of my pretty sweeting."

Then she laughed outright. "When I grow up, I will make songs, too," she said, as she stooped to pick the meadow-sweet. "I will make the words, and Rosin shall make the music; and we will go through the village singing, till everybody comes out of the houses to listen:—

Meadow-sweet is a treat;
Columbine's a fairy;
Mallow's fine, sweet as wine,—

What rhymes with fairy, I wonder. Dairy; but that won't come right. Airy, hairy,—yes, now I have it!—

Mallow's fine, sweet as wine,
To feed my pet canary.

I'll sing that to Neddy," said Melody, laughing to herself as she went along. "I can sing it to the tune of 'Lightly Row.' Dear little boy!" she added, after a silence. "Think, if he had been blind, how dreadful it would have been! Of course it doesn't matter when you have never seen at all, because you know how to get on all right; but to have it, and then lose it—oh dear! but then,"— and her face brightened again,—"he *isn't* going to be blind, you see, so what's the use of worrying about it?

> The worry cow
> Might have lived till now,
> If she'd only saved her breath.
> She thought the hay
> Wouldn't last all day,
> So she choked herself to death."

Presently the child stopped again, and listened. The sound of wheels was faintly audible. No one else could have heard it but Melody, whose ears were like those of a fox. "Whose wagon squeaks like that?" she said, as she listened. "The horse interferes, too. Oh, of course; it's Eben Loomis. He'll pick me up and give me a ride, and then it won't take so long." She walked along, turning back every now and then, as the sound of wheels came nearer and nearer. At last, "Good-morning, Eben!" she cried, smiling as the wagon drove up; "will you take me on a piece, please?"

"Wal, I might, perhaps," admitted the driver, cautiously, "if I was sure you was all right, Mel'dy. How d'you know't was me comin', I'd like to know? I never said a word, nor so much as whistled, since I come in sight of ye." The man, a wiry, yellow-haired Yankee, bent down as he spoke, and taking the child's hand, swung her lightly up to the seat beside him.

Melody laughed joyously. "I should know your wagon if I heard it in Russia, Eben," she said. "Besides, poor old Jerry knocks his hind feet together so, I heard him clicking along even before I heard the wagon squeak. How's Mandy, Eben?"

"Mandy, she ain't very well," replied the countryman. "She's ben havin' them weakly spells right along lately. Seems though she was failin' up sometimes, but I dono."

"Oh, no, she isn't, Eben," answered Melody, cheerfully. "You said that six years ago, do you know it? and Mandy isn't a bit worse than she was then."

"Well, that's so," assented the man, after a thoughtful pause. "That is so, Mel'dy, though how you come to-know it is a myst'ry to me. Come to think of it, I dono but she's a leetle mite better than she was six years ago. Wal! now it's surprising ain't it, that you should know that, you child, without the use of your eyes, and I shouldn't, seein' her every day and all day? How do you account for that, now, hey?" He turned on his seat, and looked keenly at the child, as if half expecting her to meet his gaze.

"It's easy enough!" said Melody, with her quiet smile. "It's just because you see her so much, Eben, that you can't tell. Besides, I can tell from Mandy's voice. Her voice used to go down when she stopped speaking, like this, 'How do you *do?*' [with a falling inflection which was the very essence of melancholy]; and now her voice goes up cheerfully, at the end, 'How do you do?' Don't you see the difference, Eben?—so of course I know she must be a great deal better."

"I swan!" replied Eben Loomis, simply. "'How do you *do?*' '*How* do you do?' so that's the way you find out things, is it, Mel'dy? Well, you're a curus child, that's what's the matter with you.—Where d'you say you was goin'?" he added, after a pause.

"I didn't say," said Melody. "But I'm going to Mrs. Jackson's, to see Neddy."

"Want to know," said her companion. "Goin'—Hevin' some kind o' trouble with his eyes, ain't he?" He stopped short, with a glance at the child's clear eyes. It was impossible not to expect to find some answering look in them.

"They thought he was going blind," said Melody; "but it is all right now. I do wish people wouldn't tell Mrs. Jackson to keep putting things in his eyes. Why can't they let her do what the doctor tells her, and not keep wanting her to try all kinds of nonsense?"

"Wal, that's so," assented Eben,—"that's so, every time. I was down there a spell back, and I says, 'Phoebe,' I says, 'don't you do a thing folks tells you,' says I. 'Dr. Brown knows what he's about, and don't you do a thing but what he says, unless it's jest to wet his eyes up with a drop o' tobacco-juice,' says I. 'There's nothin' like tobacco-juice for weakly eyes, that's sure;' and of course I knew Doctor would ha' said so himself ef he'd ha' been there. Wal, here we be to Jackson's now," added the good man, pulling up his horse. "Hold on a minute, and I'll help ye down. Wal, there!" as Melody sprang lightly from the wagon, just touching his hand by way of greeting as she went, "if you ain't the spryest ever I see!"

"Good-by, Eben, and thank you ever so much," said the child. "Good-by, Jerry."

"Come down an' see us, Mel'dy!" Eben called after her, as she turned toward the house with unfaltering step. "T'would do Mandy a sight o' good. Come down and stop to supper. You ain't took a meal o' victuals with us I don't know when."

Melody promised to come soon, and took her way up the grassy path, while the countryman gazed after her with a look of wondering admiration.

"That child knows more than most folks that hev their sight!" he soliloquized. "What's she doin' now? Oh, stoppin' to pick a posy, for the child, likely. Now they'll all swaller her alive. Yes; thar they come. Look at the way she takes that child up, now, will ye? He's e'en a'most as big as she is; but you'd say she was his mother ten times over, from the way she handles him. Look at her set down on the doorstep, tellin' him a story, I'll bet. I tell ye! hear that little feller laugh, and he was cryin' all last night, Mandy says. I wouldn't mind hearin' that story myself. Faculty, that gal has; that's the name for it, sir. Git up, Jerry! this won't buy the child a cake;" and with many a glance over his shoulder, the good man drove on.

CHAPTER IV.

ROSIN THE BEAU.

The afternoon light was falling soft and sweet, as an old man came slowly along the road that led to the village. He was tall and thin, and he stooped as he walked,—not with the ordinary round-shouldered slouch, but with a one-sided droop, as if he had a habit of bending over something. His white hair was fancifully arranged, with a curl over the forehead such as little boys used to wear; his brown eyes were bright and quick as a bird's, and like a bird's, they glanced from side to side, taking in everything. He carried an oblong black box, evidently a violin-case, at which he cast an affectionate look from time to time. As he approached the village, his glances became more and more keenly intelligent. He seemed to be greeting a friend in every tree, in every straggling rose-bush along the roadside; he nodded his head, and spoke softly from time to time.

"Getting on now," he said to himself. "Here's the big rose-bush she was sitting under, the last time I came along. Nobody here now; but she'll be coming directly, up from the ground or down from the sky, or through a hole in the sunset. Do you remember how she caught her little gown on that fence-rail?" He bent over, and seemed to address his violin. "Sat down and took out her needle and thread, and mended it as neat as any woman; and then ran her butterfly hands over me, and found the hole in my coat, and called me careless boy, and mended that. Yes, yes; Rosin remembers every place where he saw his girl. Old Rosin remembers. There's the turn; now it's getting time for to be playing our tune, sending our letter of introduction along the road before us. Hey?"

He sat down under a spreading elder-bush, and proceeded to open his violin-case. Drawing out the instrument with as much care as if he were a mother taking her babe from the cradle, he looked it all over with anxious scrutiny, scanning every line and crack, as the mother scans face and hands and tiny curled-up feet. Finding all in order, he wiped it with a silk handkerchief (the special property of the instrument; a cotton one did duty for himself), polished it, and tuned it, and polished again. "Must look well, my beauty," he murmured; "must look well. Not a speck of dust but she'd feel it with those little fingers, you know. Ready now? Well, then, speak up for your master; speak, voice of my heart! 'A welcome for Rosin the Beau.' Ask for it, Music!"

Do people still play "Rosin the Beau," I wonder? I asked a violinist to play it to me the other day, and he had never heard of the tune. He played me something else, which he said was very fine,—a fantasia in E flat, I think it was; but I did not care for it. I wanted to hear "Rosin the Beau," the cradle-song of the fiddle,—the sweet, simple, foolish old song, which every "blind crowder" who could handle a fiddle-bow could play in his sleep fifty years ago, and which is now wellnigh forgotten. It is not a beautiful air; it may have no merit at all, musically speaking; but I love it well, and wish I might hear it occasionally instead of the odious "Carnival of Venice," which tortures my ears and wastes my nervous system at every concert where the Queen of Instruments holds her court.

The old man took up his fiddle, and laid his cheek lovingly against it. A moment he stood still, as if holding silent commune with the spirit of music, the tricksy Ariel imprisoned in the old wooden case; then he began to play "Rosin the Beau." As he played, he kept his eyes fixed on the bend of the road some rods ahead, as if expecting every moment to see some one appear from the direction of the village.

"I've travelled this country all over,
And now to the next I must go;
But I know that good quarters await me,
And a welcome for Rosin the Beau."

As he played, with bold but tender touch, the touch of a master, round the corner a figure came flying,—a child's figure, with hair all afloat, and arms wide-opened. The old man's face lightened, softened, became transfigured with joy and love; but he said no word, only played steadily on.

"Rosin!" cried Melody, stopping close before him, with outstretched arms. "Stop, Rosin; I want to kiss you, and I am afraid of hurting her. Put her down, do you hear?" She stamped her foot imperiously, and the old man laid the fiddle down and held out his arms in turn.

"Melody," he said tenderly, taking the child on his knee,—"little Melody, how are you? So you heard old Rosin, did you? You knew the old man was here, waiting for his little maid to come and meet him, as she always has. Where were you, Melody? Tell me, now. I didn't seem to hear you till just as you came to the corner; I didn't, now."

"I was down by the heater-piece," said the child. "I went to look for wild strawberries, with Aunt Vesta. I heard you, Rosin, the moment you laid your bow across her; but Aunt Vesta said no, she knew it was all nonsense, and we'd better finish our strawberries, anyhow. And then I heard that you wondered why I didn't come, and that you wanted me, and I kissed Auntie, and just flew. You heard how fast I was coming, when you did hear me; didn't you, Rosin dear?"

"I heard," said the old man, smoothing her curls back. "I knew you'd come, you see, jewel, soon as you could get here. And how are the good ladies, hey;

and how are you yourself?—though I can tell that by looking at you, sure enough."

"Do I look well?" asked the child, with much interest. "Is my hair very nice and curly, Rosin, and do my eyes still look as if they were real eyes?" She looked up so brightly that any stranger would have been startled into thinking that she could really see.

"Bright as dollars, they are," assented the old man. "Dollars? no, that's no name for it. The stars are nearest it, Melody. And your hair—"

"My hair is like sweet Alice's," said the child, confidently,—"sweet Alice, whose hair was so brown. I promised Auntie Joy we would sing that for her, the very next time you came, but I never thought you would be here to-day, Rosin.

'Where have you been, my long, long love, this seven long years and more?'

That's a ballad, Rosin; Doctor taught it to me. It is a beauty, and you must make me a tune for it. But where *have* you been?"

"I've been up and down the earth," the old man replied,—"up and down the earth, Melody. Sometimes here and sometimes there. I'd feel a call here, and I'd feel a call there; and I seemed to be wanted, generally, just in those very places I'd felt called to. Do you believe in calls, Melody?"

"Of course I do," replied the child, promptly. "Only all the people who call you can't get you, Rosin, 'cause you'd be in fifty pieces if they did." She laughed joyously, throwing her head back with the birdlike, rapturous motion which seemed the very expression of her nature.

The old fiddler watched her with delight. "You shall hear all my stories," he said; "everything you shall hear, little Melody; but here we are at the house now, and I must make my manners to the ladies."

He paused, and looked critically at his blue coat, which, though threadbare, was scrupulously clean. He flecked some imaginary dust from his trousers, and ran his hand lightly through his hair, bringing the snowy curl which was the pride of his heart a little farther over his forehead. "Now I'll do, maybe," he said cheerfully. "And sure enough, there's Miss Vesta in the doorway, looking like a China rose in full bloom." He advanced, hat in hand, with a peculiar sliding step, which instantly suggested "chassez across to partners."

"Miss Vesta, I hope your health's good?"

Miss Vesta held out her hand cordially. "Why, Mr. De Arthenay, [Footnote: Pronounced Dee arthenay] is this you?" she cried. "This is a pleasure! Melody was sure it was you, and she ran off like a will-o'-the-wisp, when I could not hear a sound. But I'm very glad to see you. We were saying only yesterday how long a time it was since you'd been here. Now you must sit down, and tell us all the news. Stop, though," she added, with a glance at the vine-clad window; "Rejoice would like to see you, and hear the news too. Wait a moment, Mr. De Arthenay! I'll go in and move her up by the window, so that she can hear you."

She hastened into the house; and in a few minutes the blinds were thrown back, and Miss Rejoice's sweet voice was heard, saying, "Good-day, Mr. De Arthenay. It is always a good day that brings you."

The old man sprang up from his seat in the porch, and made a low bow to the window. "It's a treat to hear your voice, Miss Rejoice, so it is," he said heartily. "I hope your health's been pretty good lately? It seems to me your voice sounds stronger than it did the last time I was here."

"Oh, I'm very well," responded the invalid, cheerfully. "Very well, I feel this summer; don't I, Vesta? And where have you been, Mr. De Arthenay, all this time? I'm sure you have a great deal to tell us. It's as good as a newspaper when you come along, we always say."

The old fiddler cleared his throat, and settled himself comfortably in a corner of the porch, with Melody's hand in his. Miss Vesta produced her knitting; Melody gave a little sigh of perfect content, and nestled up to her friend's side, leaning her head against his shoulder.

"Begin to tell now, Rosin," she said. "Tell us all that you know."

"Tell you everything," he repeated thoughtfully. "Not all, little Melody. I've seen some things that you wouldn't like to hear about,—things that would grieve your tender heart more than a little. We will not talk about those; but I have seen bright things too, sure enough. Why, only day before yesterday I was at a wedding, over in Pegrum; a pretty wedding it was too. You remember Myra Bassett, Miss Vesta?"

"To be sure I do," replied Miss Vesta. "She married John Andrews, her father's second cousin once removed. Don't tell me that Myra has a daughter old enough to be married: Or is it a son? either way, it is ridiculous."

"A daughter!" said the old man,—"the prettiest girl in Pegrum. Like a ripe chestnut, more than anything. Two lads were in love with her; there may have been a dozen, but these two I know about. One of them—I'll name no names, 'tis kinder not—found that she wanted to marry a hero (what girl does not?), so he thought he would try his hand at heroism. There was a picnic this spring, and he hired a boy (or so the boy says—it may be wicked gossip) to upset the boat she was in, so that he, the lover, might save her life. But, lo and behold! he was taken with a cramp in the water, and was almost drowned, and the second lover jumped in, and saved them both. So she married the second (whom she had liked all along), and then the boy told his story."

"Miserable sneak!" ejaculated Miss Vesta. "To risk the life of the woman he pretended to love, just to show himself off."

"Still, I am sorry for him!" said Miss Rejoice, through the window. (Miss Rejoice was always sorry for wrongdoers, much sorrier than for the righteous who suffered. *They* would be sure to get good out of it, she said, but the poor sinners generally didn't know how.) "What did he do, poor soul?"

"He went away!" replied the fiddler. "Pegrum wouldn't hold him; and the other lad was a good shot, and went about with a shot-gun. But I was going to tell you about the wedding."

"Of course!" cried Melody. "What did the bride wear? That is the most important part."

De Arthenay cleared his throat, and looked grave. He always made a point of remembering the dresses at weddings, and was proud of the accomplishment,—a rare one in his sex.

"Miss Andrews—I beg her pardon, Mrs. Nelson—had on a white muslin gown, made quite full, with three ruffles round the skirt. There was lace round the neck, but I cannot tell you what kind, except that it was very soft and fine. She had white roses on the front of her gown, and in her hair, and pink ones in her cheeks; her eyes were like brown diamonds, and she had little white satin slippers, for all the world like Cinderella. They were a present from her Grandmother Anstey, over at Bow Mills. Her other grandmother, Mrs. Bowen, gave her the dress, so her father and mother could lay out all they wanted to on the supper; and a handsome supper it was. Then after supper they danced. It would have done your heart good, Miss Vesta, to see that little bride dance. Ah! she is a pretty creature. There was another young woman, too, who played the piano. Kate, they called her, but I don't know what her other name was. Anyway, she had an eye like black lightning stirred up with a laugh, and a voice like the 'Fisherman's Hornpipe.'"

He took up his fiddle, and softly, delicately, played a few bars of that immortal dance. It rippled like a woman's laugh, and Melody smiled in instant sympathy.

"I wish I had seen her," she cried. "Did she play well, Rosin?"

"She played so that I knew she must be either French or Irish!" the fiddler replied. "No Yankee ever played dance-music in that fashion; I made bold to say to her, as we were playing together, 'Etes-vous compatriote?'"

"'More power to your elbow,' said she, with a twinkle of her eye, and she struck into 'Saint Patrick's Day in the Morning.' I took it up, and played the 'Marseillaise,' over it and under it, and round it,—for an accompaniment, you understand, Melody; and I can tell you, we made the folks open their eyes. Yes; she was a fine young lady, and it was a fine wedding altogether.

"But I am forgetting a message I have for you, ladies. Last week I was passing through New Joppa, and I stopped to call on Miss Lovina Green; I always stop there when I go through that region. Miss Lovina asked me to tell you— let me see! what was it?" He paused, to disentangle this particular message from the many he always carried, in his journeyings from one town to another. "Oh, yes, I remember. She wanted you to know that her Uncle Reuel was dead, and had left her a thousand dollars, so she should be comfortable the rest of her days. She thought you'd be glad to know it."

"That is good news!" exclaimed Miss Vesta, heartily. "Poor Lovina! she has been so straitened all these years, and saw no prospect of anything better. The best day's work Reuel Green has ever done was to die and leave that money to Lovina."

"Why, Vesta!" said Miss Rejoice's soft voice; "how you do talk!"

"Well, it's true!" Miss Vesta replied. "And you know it, Rejoice, my dear, as well as I do. Any other news in Joppa, Mr. De Arthenay? I haven't heard from over there for a long time."

"Why, they've been having some robberies in Joppa," the old man said,— "regular burglaries. There's been a great excitement about it. Several houses have been entered and robbed, some of money, others of what little silver there was, though I don't suppose there is enough silver in all New Joppa to support a good, healthy burglar for more than a few days. The funny part of it is that though I have no house, I came very near being robbed myself."

"You, Rosin?"

"You, Mr. De Arthenay? Do tell us!"

Melody passed her hand rapidly over the old man's face, and then settled back with her former air of content, knowing that all was well.

"You shall hear my story," the old man said, drawing himself up, and giving his curl a toss. "It was the night I came away from Joppa. I had been taking tea with William Bradwell's folks, and stayed rather late in the evening, playing for the young folks, singing old songs, and one thing and another. It was ten o'clock when I said good-night and stepped out of the house and along the road. 'T was a fine night, bright moonlight, and everything shining like silver. I'd had a pleasant evening, and I felt right cheered up as I passed along, sometimes talking a bit to the Lady, and sometimes she to me; for I'd left her case at the house, seeing I should pass by again in the morning, when I took my way out of the place.

"Well, sir,—I beg your pardon; *ladies*, I should say,—as I came along a strip of the road with the moon full on it, but bordered with willow scrub,—as I came along, sudden a man stepped out of those bushes, and told me to stand and throw up my hands.—Don't be frightened, Melody," for the child had taken his hand with a quick, frightened motion; "have no fear at all! I had none. I saw, or felt, perhaps it was, that he had no pistols; that he was only a poor sneak and bully. So I said, 'Stand yourself!' I stepped clear out, so that the light fell full on my face, and I looked him in the eye, and pointed my bow at him. 'My name is De Arthenay,' I said. 'I am of French extraction, but I hail from the Androscoggin. I am known in this country. This is my fiddle-bow; and if you are not gone before I can count three, I'll shoot you with it. One!' I said; but I didn't need to count further. He turned and ran, as if the— as if a regiment was after him; and as soon as I had done laughing, I went on my way to the tavern."

All laughed heartily at the old man's story; but when the laughter subsided, Melody begged him to take "the Lady," and play for her. "I have not heard you play for so long, Rosin, except just when you called me."

"Yes, Mr. De Arthenay," said Miss Vesta, "do play a little for us, while I get supper. Suppose I bring the table out here, Melody; how would you like that?"

"Oh, so much!" cried the child, clapping her hands. "So very much! Let me help!"

She started up; and while the fiddler played, old sweet melodies, such as Miss Rejoice loved, there was a pleasant, subdued bustle of coming and going, clinking and rustling, as the little table was brought out and set in the vine-wreathed porch, the snowy cloth laid, and the simple feast set forth. There were wild strawberries, fresh and glowing, laid on vine-leaves; there were biscuits so light it seemed as if a puff of wind might blow them away; there were twisted doughnuts, and coffee brown and as clear as a mountain brook. It was a pleasant little feast; and the old fiddler glanced with cheerful approval over the table as he sat down.

"Ah, Miss Vesta," he said, as he handed the biscuits gallantly to his hostess, "there's no such table as this for me to sit down to, wherever I go, far or near. Look at the biscuit, now,—moulded snow, I call them. Take one, Melody, my dear. You'll never get anything better to eat in this world."

The child flushed with pleasure.

"You're praising her too much to herself," said Miss Vesta, with a pleased smile. "Melody made those biscuit, all herself, without any help. She's getting to be such a good housekeeper, Mr. De Arthenay, you would not believe it."

"You don't tell me that she made these biscuit!" cried the old man. "Why, Melody, I shall be frightened at you if you go on at this rate. You are not growing up, are you, little Melody?"

"No! no! no!" cried the child, vehemently. "I am *not* growing up, Rosin. I don't want to grow up, ever, at all."

"I should like to know what you can do about it," said Miss Vesta, smiling grimly. "You'll have to stop pretty short if you are not going to grow up, Melody. If I have let your dresses down once this spring, I've let them down three times. You're going to be a tall woman, I should say, and you've a right good start toward it now."

A shade stole over the child's bright face, and she was silent,—seeming only half to listen while the others chatted, yet never forgetting to serve them, and seeming, by a touch on the hand of either friend, to know what was wanted.

When the meal was over, and the tea-things put away, Melody came out again into the porch, where the fiddler sat smoking his pipe, and leaning against one of the supports, felt among the leaves which hid it. "Here is the mark!" she said. "Am I really taller, Rosin? Really much taller?"

"What troubles the child?" the old man asked gently. "She does not want to grow? The bud must open, Melody, my dear! the bud must open!"

"But it's so unreasonable," cried Melody, as she stood holding by the old man's hand, swaying lightly to and fro, as if the wind moved her with the vines and flowers. "Why can't I stay a little girl? A little girl is needed here, isn't she? And there is no need at all of another woman. I can't be like Aunt Vesta or Auntie Joy; so I think I might stay just Melody." Then shaking her curls back, she cried, "Well, anyhow, I am just Melody now, and nothing more; and I mean to make the most of it. Come, Rosin, come! I am ready for music. The dishes are all washed, and there's nothing more to do, is there, Auntie? It is so long since Rosin has been here; now let us have a good time, a perfect time!"

De Arthenay took up his fiddle once more, and caressed its shining curves. "She's in perfect trim," he said tenderly. "She's fit to play with you to-night, Melody. Come, I am ready; what shall we have?"

Melody sat down on the little green bench which was her own particular seat. She folded her hands lightly on her lap, and threw her head back with her own birdlike gesture. One would have said that she was calling the spirit of song, which might descend on rainbow wings, and fold her in his arms. The

old man drew the bow softly, and the fiddle gave out a low, brooding note,—
a note of invitation.

"Oh, don't you remember sweet Alice, Ben Bolt?
Sweet Alice, whose hair was so brown?
She wept with delight when you gave her a smile,
And trembled with fear at your frown."

Softly the old man played, keeping his eyes fixed on the child, whose glorious
voice floated out on the evening air, filling the whole world with sweetest
melody. Miss Vesta dropped her knitting and folded her hands, while a
peaceful, dreamy look stole into her fine face,—a face whose only fault was
the too eager look which a New England woman must so often gain, whether
she will or no. In the quiet chamber, the bedridden woman lay back on her
pillows smiling, with a face as the face of an angel. Her thoughts were lifted
up on the wings of the music, and borne—who shall say where, to what high
and holy presence? Perhaps—who can tell?—the eyes of her soul looked in
at the gate of heaven itself; if it were so, be sure they saw nothing within that
white portal more pure and clear than their own gaze.

And still the song flowed on. Presently doors began to open along the village
street. People came softly out, came on tiptoe toward the cottage, and with a
silent greeting to its owner sat down beside the road to listen. Children came
dancing, with feet almost as light as Melody's own, and curled themselves up
beside her on the grass. Tired-looking mothers came, with their babies in
their arms; and the weary wrinkles faded from their faces, and they listened
in silent content, while the little ones, who perhaps had been fretting and
complaining a moment before, nestled now quietly against the mother-breast,
and felt that no one wanted to tease or ill-treat them, but that the world was
all full of Mother, who loved them. Beside one of these women a man came
and sat him down, as if from habit; but he did not look at her. His face wore
a weary, moody frown, and he stared at the ground sullenly, taking no note
of any one. The others looked at one another and nodded, and thought of
the things they knew; the woman cast a sidelong glance at him, half hopeful,
half fearful, but made no motion.

"Oh, don't you remember the school, Ben Bolt,
And the master so kind and so true;
And the little nook by the clear running brook,
Where we gathered the flowers as they grew?"

The dark-browed man listened, and thought. Her name was Alice, this
woman by his side. They had been schoolmates together, had gathered
flowers, oh, how many times, by brook-side and hill. They had grown up to
be lovers, and she was his wife, sitting here now beside him,—his wife, with
his baby in her arms; and he had not spoken to her for a week. What began

it all? He hardly knew; but she had been provoking, and he had been tired, impatient; there had been a great scene, and then this silence, which he swore he would not break. How sad she looked! he thought, as he stole a glance at the face bending over the child.

"Oh, don't you remember sweet Alice, Ben Bolt,
   Sweet Alice, whose hair was so brown?"

Was she singing about them, this child? She had sung at their wedding, a little thing of seven years old; and old De Arthenay had played, and wished them happiness, and said they were the handsomest couple he had played for that year. Now she looked so tired: how was it that he had never seen how tired she looked? Perhaps she was only sick or nervous that day when she spoke so. The child stirred in its mother's arms, and she gave a low sigh of weariness, and shifted the weight to the other arm. The young man bent forward and took the baby, and felt how heavy it had grown since last he held it. He had not said anything, he would not say anything—just yet; but his wife turned to him with such a smile, such a flash of love and joy, imploring, promising, that his heart leaped, and then beat peacefully, happily, as it had not beaten for many days. All was over; and Alice leaned against his arm with a little movement of content, and the good neighbors looked at one another again, and smiled this time to know that all was well.

What is the song now? The blind child turns slightly, so that she faces Miss Vesta Dale, whose favorite song this is,—

"All in the merry month of May,
   When green buds were a-swellin",
Young Jemmy Grove on his death-bed lay,
   For love of Barbara Allan."

Why is Miss Vesta so fond of the grim old ballad? Perhaps she could hardly tell, if she would. She looks very stately as she leans against the wall, close by the room where her sister Rejoice is lying. Does a thought come to her mind of the youth who loved her so, or thought he loved her, long and long ago? Does she see his look of dismay, of incredulous anger, when she told him that her life must be given to her crippled sister, and that if he would share it he must take Rejoice too, to love and to cherish as dearly as he would cherish her? He could not bear the test; he was a good young fellow enough, but there was nothing of the hero about him, and he thought that crippled folk should be taken care of in hospitals, where they belonged.

"'Oh, dinna ye mind, young man,' she said,
   'When the redl wine was a-fillin',
Ye bade the healths gae round an' round,
   And slighted Barbara Allan?'"

If the cruel Barbara had not repented, and "laid her down in sorrow," she might well have grown to look like this handsome, white-haired woman, with her keen blue eyes and queenly bearing.

Miss Vesta had never for an instant regretted the disposition of her life, never even in the shadow of a thought; but this was the song she used to sing in those old days, and somehow she always felt a thrill (was it of pleasure or pain? she could not have told you) when the child sang it.

But there may have been a "call," as Rosin the Beau would have said, for some one else beside Vesta Dale; for a tall, pale girl, who has been leaning against the wall pulling off the gray lichens as she listened, now slips away, and goes home and writes a letter; and to-morrow morning, when the mail goes to the next village, two people will be happy in God's world instead of being miserable. And now? Oh, now it is a merry song; for, after all, Melody is a child, and a happy child; and though she loves the sad songs dearly, still she generally likes to end up with a "dancy one."

"'Come boat me o'er,
Come row me o'er,
Come boat me o'er to Charlie;
I'll gi'e John Ross anither bawbee
To boat me o'er to Charlie.
We'll o'er the water an' o'er the sea,
We'll o'er the water to Charlie,
Come weal, come woe, we'll gather and go,
And live and die wi' Charlie.'"

And now Rosin the Beau proves the good right he has to his name. Trill and quavers and roulades are shaken from his bow as lightly as foam from the prow of a ship. The music leaps rollicking up and down, here and there, till the air is all a-quiver with merriment. The old man draws himself up to his full height, all save that loving bend of the head over the beloved instrument. His long slender foot, in its quaint "Congress" shoe, beats time like a mill-clapper,—tap, tap, tap; his snowy curl dances over his forehead, his brown eyes twinkle with pride and pleasure. Other feet beside his began to pat the ground; heads were lifted, eyes looked invitation and response. At length the child Melody, with one superb outburst of song, lifted her hands above her head, and springing out into the road cried, "A dance! a dance!"

Instantly the quiet road was alive with dancers. Old and young sprang to their feet in joyful response. The fiddle struck into "The Irish Washerwoman," and the people danced. Children joined hands and jumped up and down, knowing no steps save Nature's leaps of joy; youths and maidens flew in graceful measures together; last, but not least, old Simon Parker the postmaster seized Mrs. Martha Penny by both hands, and regardless of her breathless shrieks whirled her round and round till the poor old dame had no breath left to scream with. Alone in the midst of the gay throng (as strange a one, surely, as ever disturbed the quiet of a New England country road) danced the blind child, a figure of perfect grace. Who taught Melody to dance? Surely it was the wind, the swaying birch-tree, the slender grasses that nod and wave by the brookside. Light as air she floated in and out among the motley groups, never jostling or touching any one. Her slender arms waved in time to the music; her beautiful hair floated over her shoulders. Her whole face glowed with light and joy, while only her eyes, steadfast and unchanging, struck the one grave note in the symphony of joy and merriment.

From time to time the old fiddler stole a glance at Miss Vesta Dale, as she sat erect and stately, leaning against the wall of the house. She was beginning to grow uneasy. Her foot also began to pat the ground. She moved slightly, swayed on her seat; her fingers beat time, as did the slender, well-shaped foot which peeped from under her scant blue skirt. Suddenly De Arthenay stopped short, and tapped sharply on his fiddle, while the dancers, breathless and exhausted, fell back by the roadside again. Stepping out from the porch, he made a low bow to Miss Vesta. "Chorus Jig!" he cried, and struck up the air of that time-honored dance. Miss Vesta frowned, shook her head resolutely,—rose, and standing opposite the old fiddler, began to dance.

Here was a new marvel, no less strange in its way than Melody's wild grace of movement, or the sudden madness of the village crowd. The stately white-haired woman moved slowly forward; the old man bowed again; she courtesied as became a duchess of Nature's own making. Their bodies erect and motionless, their heads held high, their feet went twinkling through a series of evolutions which the keenest eye could hardly follow. "Pigeon-wings?" Whole flocks of pigeons took flight from under that scant blue skirt, from those wonderful shrunken trousers of yellow nankeen. They moved forward, back, forward again, as smoothly as a wave glides up the shore. They twinkled round and round each other, now back to back, now face to face. They chasséd into corners, and displayed a whirlwind of delicately pointed toes; they retired as if to quarrel; they floated back to make it up again. All the while not a muscle of their faces moved, not a gleam of fun disturbed the tranquil sternness of their look; for dancing was a serious business thirty years ago, when they were young, and they had no idea of lowering its dignity by any "quips and cranks and wanton wiles," such as young folks nowadays indulge in. Briefly, it was a work of art; and when it was over, and the sweeping courtesy and splendid bow had restored the old-time dancers to their places, a shout of applause went up, and the air rang with such a tumult as had never before, perhaps, disturbed the tranquillity of the country road.

CHAPTER V.

IN THE CHURCHYARD.

God's Acre! A New England burying-ground,—who does not know the aspect of the place? A savage plot of ground, where nothing else would grow save this crop of gray stones, and other gray stones formless and grim, thrusting their rugged faces out here and there through the scanty soil. Other stones, again, enclosing the whole with a grim, protecting arm, a ragged wall, all jagged, formless, rough. The grass is long and yet sparse; here and there a few flowers cling, hardy geraniums, lychnis, and the like, but they seem strangely out of place. The stones are fallen awry, and lean toward each other as if they exchanged confidences, and speculated on the probable spiritual whereabouts of the souls whose former bodies they guard. Most of these stones are gray slate, carved with old-fashioned letters, round and long-tailed; but there are a few slabs of white marble, and in one corner is a marble lamb, looking singularly like the woolly lambs one buys for children, standing stiff and solemn on his four straight legs. This is not the "cemetery," be it understood. That is close by the village, and is the favorite walk and place of Sunday resort for its inhabitants. It is trim and well-kept, with gravel paths and flower-beds, and store of urns and images in "white bronze," for the people are proud of their cemetery, as well-regulated New England people should be, and there is a proper feeling of rivalry in the matter of "moniments."

But Melody cares nothing whatever about the fine cemetery. It is in the old "berrin'-groun'" that her mother lies,—indeed, she was the last person buried in it; and it is here that the child loves to linger and dream the sweet, sad, purposeless dreams of childhood. She knows nothing of "Old Mortality," yet she is his childish imitator in this lonely spot. She keeps the weeds in some sort of subjection; she pulls away the moss and lichens from head and foot stones,—not so much with any idea of reverence as that she likes to read the inscriptions, and feel the quaint flourishes and curlicues of the older gravestones. She has a sense of personal acquaintance with all the dwellers on this hillside; talks to them and sings to them in her happy fashion, as she pulls away the witch-grass and sorrel. See her now, sitting on that low green mound, her white dress gleaming against the dusky gray of the stone on which she leans. Melody is very fond of white. It feels smoother than colors, she always says; and she would wear it constantly if it did not make too much washing. One arm is thrown over the curve of the headstone, while with the other hand she follows the worn letters of the inscription, which surely no other fingers were fine enough to trace.

SACRED TO THE MEMORY OF

SUSAN DYER.

TRUE TO HER NAME,

She died Aug. 10th, 1814,
  In the 19th year of her age.

The soul of my Susan is gone
  To heighten the triumphs above;
Exalted to Jesus's throne
  And clasped in the arms of his love.

Melody read the words aloud, smiling as she read. "Susan," she said, "I wonder who wrote your verses. I wonder if you were pretty, dear, and if you liked to be alive, and were sorry to be dead. But you must be used to it by this time, anyhow. I wonder if you 'shout redeeming love,' like your cousin (I suppose she is your cousin) Sophia Dyer, over in the corner there. I never liked Sophia, Susan dear. I seem to think she shouted here too, and snubbed you, because you were gentle and shy. See how her stone perks up, making every inch it can of itself, while yours tries to sink away and hide itself in the good green grass. I think we liked the same things a good deal, Susan, don't you? And I think you would like me to go and see the old gentleman now, because he has so many dandelions; and I really must pull them up. You know I am never sure that he isn't your grandfather. So many of you are related here, it is a regular family party. Good-by, Susan dear."

She bent over, and touched the stone lightly with her lips, then passed on to another which was half buried in the earth, the last letters of the inscription being barely discernible.

"How do you do, Mr. Bascom?" said this singular child, laying her hand respectfully on the venerable headstone. "Are your dandelions very troublesome this morning, dear sir?"

Her light fingers hovered over the mound like butterflies, and she began pulling up the dandelion roots, and smoothing down the grass over the bare places. Then she fell to work on the inscription, which was an elaborate one, surmounted by two cherubs' heads, one resting on an hour-glass, the other on a pair of cross-bones. Along every line she passed her delicate fingers, not because she did not know every line, but that she might trace any new growth of moss or lichen.

"Farewell this flesh, these ears, these eyes,
  Those snares and fetters of the mind

My God, nor let this frame arise
  Till every dust be well refined."

"You were very particular, Mr. Bascom, weren't you?" inquired Melody. "You were a very neat old gentleman, with white hair always brushed just so, and a high collar. You didn't like dust, unless it was well refined. I shouldn't wonder if you washed your walking-stick every time you came home, like Mr. Cuter, over at the Corners. Here's something growing in the tail of your last *y*. Never mind, Mr. Bascom, I'll get it out with a pin. There, now you are quite respectable, and you look very nice indeed. Good-by, and do try not to fret more than you can help about the dandelions. They will grow, no matter how often I come."

Melody, in common with most blind persons, always spoke of seeing, of looking at things, precisely as if she had the full use of her eyes. Indeed, I question whether those wonderful fingers of hers were not as good as many pairs of eyes we see. How many people go half-blind through the world, just for want of the habit of looking at things! How many plod onward, with eyes fixed on the ground, when they might be raised to the skies, seeing the glory of the Lord, which He has spread abroad over hill and meadow, for all eyes to behold! How many walk with introverted gaze, seeing only themselves, while their neighbor walks beside them, unseen, and needing their ministration!

The blind child touched life with her hand, and knew it. Every leaf was her acquaintance, every flower her friend and gossip. She knew every tree of the forest by its bark; knew when it blossomed, and how. More than this,—some subtle sense for which we have no name gave her the power of reading with a touch the mood and humor of those she was with; and when her hand rested in that of a friend, she knew whether the friend were glad or gay, before hearing the sound of his voice.

Another power she had,—that of attracting to her "all creatures living beneath the sun, that creep or swim or fly or run." Not a cat or dog in the village but would leave his own master or mistress at a single call from Melody. She could imitate every bird-call with her wonderful voice; and one day she had come home and told Miss Rejoice quietly that she had been making a concert with a wood-thrush, and that the red squirrels had sat on the branches to listen. Miss Vesta said, "Nonsense, child! you fell asleep, and had a pretty dream." But Miss Rejoice believed every word, and Melody knew she did by the touch of her thin, kind old hand.

It might well have been true; for now, as the child sat down beside a small white stone, which evidently marked a child's grave, she gave a low call, and in a moment a gray squirrel came running from the stone wall (he had been sitting there, watching her with his bright black eyes, looking so like a bit of the wall itself that the sharpest eyes would hardly have noticed him), and leaped into her lap.

"Brother Gray-frock, how do you do?" cried the child, joyously, caressing the pretty creature with light touches. "I wondered if I should see you to-day, brother. The last time I came you were off hunting somewhere, and I called and called, but no gray brother came. How is the wife, and the children, and how is the stout young man?"

The "stout young man" lay buried at the farther end of the ground, under the tree in which the squirrel lived. The inscription on his tombstone was a perpetual amusement to Melody, and she could not help feeling as if the squirrel must know that it was funny too, though they had never exchanged remarks about it. This was the inscription:

"I was a stout young man
As you would find in ten;
And when on this I think,
I take in hand my pen
And write it plainly out,
That all the world may see
How I was cut down like
A blossom from a tree.
The Lord rest my soul."

The young man's name was Faithful Parker. Melody liked him well enough, though she never felt intimate with him, as she did with Susan Dyer and the dear child Love Good, who slept beneath this low white stone. This was Melody's favorite grave. It was such a dear quaint little name,—Love Good. "Good" had been a common name in the village seventy years ago, when this little Love lived and died; many graves bore the name, though no living person now claimed it.

LOVE GOOD,

FOUR YEARS OLD.

Our white rose withered in the bud.

This was all; and somehow Melody felt that she knew and cared for these parents much more than for those who put their sorrow into rhyme, and mourned in despairing doggerel.

Melody laid her soft warm cheek against the little white stone, and murmured loving words to it. The squirrel sat still in her lap, content to nestle under her hand, and bask in the light and warmth of the summer day: the sunlight streamed with tempered glow through the branches of an old cedar that grew beside the little grave; peace and silence brooded like a dove over the holy place.

A flutter of wings, a rustle of leaves,—was it a fairy alighting on the old cedar-tree? No, only an oriole; though some have said that this bird is a fairy prince in disguise, and that if he can win the love of a pure maiden the spell will be loosed, and he will regain his own form. This cannot be true, however; for Melody knows Golden Robin well, and loves him well, and he loves her in his own way, yet has never changed a feather at sight of her. He will sing for her, though; and sing he does, shaking and trilling and quivering, pouring his little soul out in melody for joy of the summer day, and of the sweet, quiet place, and of the child who never scares or startles him, only smiles, and sings to him in return. They are singing together now, the child and the bird. It is a very wonderful thing, if there were any one by to hear. The gray squirrel crouches motionless in the child's lap, with half-shut eyes; the quiet dead sleep on unmoved: who else should be near to listen to such music as this?

Nay, but who is this, leaning over the old stone-wall, listening with keenest interest,—this man with the dark, eager face and bold black eyes? His eyes are fixed on the child; his face is aglow with wonder and delight, but with something else too,—some passion which strikes a jarring note through the harmony of the summer idyl. What is this man doing here? Why does he eye the blind child so strangely, with looks of power, almost of possession?

Cease, cease your song, Melody! Fly, bird and tiny beast, to your shelter in the dark tree-tops; and fly you also, gentlest child, to the home where is love and protection and tender care! For the charm is broken, and your paradise is invaded.

CHAPTER VI.

THE SERPENT.

"But I'm sure you will listen to reason, ma'am."

The stranger spoke in a low, persuasive tone; his eyes glanced rapidly hither and thither as he spoke, taking the bearings of house and garden, noting the turn of the road, the distance of the neighboring houses. One would have said he was a surveyor, only he had no instruments with him.

"I am sure you will listen to reason,—a fine, intelligent lady like yourself. Think of it: there is a fortune in this child's voice. There hasn't been such a voice—there's never been such a voice in this country, I'll be bold to say. I know something about voices, ma'am. I've been in the concert business twenty years, and I do assure you I have never heard such a natural voice as this child has. She has a great career before her, I tell you. Money, ma'am! there's thousands in that voice! It sings bank-notes and gold-pieces, every note of it. You'll be a rich woman, and she will be a great singer,—one of the very greatest. Her being blind makes it all the better. I wouldn't have her like other people, not for anything. The blind prima-donna,—my stars! wouldn't it draw? I see the posters now. 'Nature's greatest marvel, the blind singer! Splendid talent enveloped in darkness.' She will be the success of the day, ma'am. Lord, and to think of my chancing on her here, of all the little out-of-the-way places in the world! Why, three hours ago I was cursing my luck, when my horse lost a shoe and went lame, just outside your pleasant little town here. And now, ma'am, now I count this the most fortunate day of my life! Is the little lady in the house, ma'am? I'd like to have a little talk with her; kind o' open her eyes to what's before her,—her mind's eye, Horatio, eh? Know anything of Shakspeare, ma'am? Is she in the house, I say?"

"She is not," said Miss Vesta Dale, finding her voice at last. "The child is away, and you should not see her if she were here. She is not meant for the sort of thing you talk about. She—she is the same as our own child, my sister's and mine. We mean to keep her by us as long as we live. I thank you," she added, with stately courtesy. "I don't doubt that many might be glad of such a chance, but we are not that kind, my sister and I."

The man's face fell; but the next moment he looked incredulous. "You don't mean what you say, ma'am!" he cried; "you can't mean it! To keep a voice like that shut up in a God-forsaken little hole like this,—oh, you don't know what you're talking about, really you don't.' And think of the advantage to the child herself!" He saw the woman's face change at this, saw that he had made a point, and hastened to pursue it. "What can the child have, if she spends her life here? No education, no pleasure,—nothing. Nice little place, no doubt, for those that are used to it, but—Lord! a child that has the whole world before her, to pick and choose! She must go to Europe, ma'am! She will sing before crowned heads; go to Russia, and be decorated by the Czar. She'll have horses and carriages, jewels, dresses finer than any queen! Patti spends three fortunes a year on her clothes, and this girl has as good a voice as Patti, any day. Why, you have to support her, don't you?—and hard work, too, sometimes, perhaps—her and maybe others?"

Miss Vesta winced; and he saw it. Oh, Rejoice! it was a joy to save and spare, to deny herself any little luxury, that the beloved sister might have everything she fancied. But did she have everything? Was it, could it be possible that this should be done for her sister's sake?

The man pursued his advantage relentlessly. "You are a fine woman, ma'am, if you'll allow me to say so,—a remarkably fine woman. But you are getting on in life, as we all are. This child will support you, ma'am, instead of your supporting her. Support you, do I say? Why, you'll be rolling in wealth in a few years! You spoke of a sister, ma'am. Is she in good health, may I ask?" His quick eye had spied the white-curtained bed through the vine-clad window, and his ear had caught the tender tone of her voice when she said, "my sister."

"My sister is an invalid," said Miss Vesta, coldly.

"Another point!" exclaimed the impresario. "You will be able to have every luxury for your sister,—wines, fruits, travelling, the best medical aid the country affords. You are the—a—the steward, I may say, ma'am,"—with subtle intuition, the man assumed a tone of moral loftiness, as if calling Miss Vesta to account for all delinquencies, past and future,—"the steward, or even the stewardess, of this great treasure. It means everything for you and her, and for your invalid sister as well. Think of it, think of it well! I am so confident of your answer that I can well afford to wait a little. Take a few minutes, ma'am, and think it over."

He leaned against the house in an easy attitude, with his hands in his pockets, and his mouth pursed up for a whistle. He did not feel as confident as he looked, perhaps, but Miss Vesta did not know that. She also leaned against the house, her head resting among the vines that screened Miss Rejoice's window, and thought intensely. What was right? What should she do? Half an hour ago life lay so clear and plain before her; the line of happy duties, simple pleasures, was so straight, leading from the cottage door to that quiet spot in the old burying-ground where she and Rejoice would one day rest side by side. They had taught Melody what they could. She had books in raised print, sent regularly from the institution where she had learned to read and write. She was happy; no child could ever have been happier, Miss Vesta thought, if she had had three pairs of eyes. She was the heart of the village, its pride, its wonder. They had looked forward to a life of simple usefulness and kindliness for her, tending the sick with that marvellous skill which seemed a special gift from Heaven; cheering, comforting, delighting old and young, by the magic of her voice and the gentle spell of her looks and ways. A quiet life, a simple, humdrum life, it might be: they had never thought of that. But now, what picture was this that the stranger had conjured up?

As in a glass, Miss Vesta seemed to see the whole thing. Melody a woman, a great singer, courted, caressed, living like a queen, with everything rich and beautiful about her; jewels in her shining hair, splendid dresses, furs and laces, such as even elderly country women love to dream about sometimes. She saw this; and she saw something else besides. The walls of the little room within seemed to part, to extend; it was no longer a tiny whitewashed closet, but stretched wide and long, rose lofty and airy. There were couches, wheeled chairs, great sunny windows, through which one looked out over lovely gardens; there were pictures, the most beautiful in the world, for those dear eyes to rest on; banks of flowers, costly ornaments, everything that luxury could devise or heart desire. And on one of these splendid couches (oh, she could move as she pleased from one to the other, instead of lying always in the one narrow white bed!),—on one of them lay her sister Rejoice, in a lace wrapper, such as Miss Vesta had read about once in a fashion magazine; all lace, creamy and soft, with delicate ribbons here and there. There she lay; and yet—was it she? Miss Vesta tried hard to give life to this image, to make it smile with her sister's eyes, and speak with her sister's voice; but it had a strange, shadowy look all the time, and whenever she forced the likeness of Rejoice into her mind, somehow it came with the old surroundings, the little white bed, the yellow-washed walls, the old green flag-bottomed chair on which the medicine-cups always stood. But all the other things might be hers, just by Melody's singing. By Melody's singing! Miss Vesta stood very still, her face quiet and stern, as it always was in thought, no sign of the struggle going on within. The stranger was very still too, biding his time, stealing an occasional glance at her face, feeling tolerably sure of success, yet wishing she had not quite such a set look about the mouth.

All by Melody's singing! No effort, no exertion for the child, only the thing she loved best in the world,—the thing she did every day and all day. And all for Rejoice, for Rejoice, whom Melody loved so; for whom the child would count any toil, any privation, merely an added pleasure, even as Vesta herself would. Miss Vesta held her breath, and prayed. Would not God answer for her? She was only a woman, and very weak, though she had never guessed it till now. God knew what the right thing was: would He not speak for her?

She looked up, and saw Melody coming down the road, leading a child in each hand. She was smiling, and the children were laughing, though there were traces of tears on their cheeks; for they had been quarrelling when Melody found them in the fields and brought them away. It was a pretty picture; the stranger's eyes brightened as he gazed at it. But for the first time in her life Miss Vesta was not glad to see Melody. The child began to sing, and the woman listened for the words, with a vague trouble darkening over her perturbed spirit as a thunder-cloud comes blackening a gray sky, filling it with angry mutterings, with quick flashes. What if the child should sing the wrong words, she thought! What were the wrong words, and how should she know whether they were of God or the Devil?

It was an old song that Melody was singing; she knew few others, indeed,— only the last verse of an old song, which Vesta Dale had heard all her life, and had never thought much about, save that it was a good song, one of the kind Rejoice liked.

"There's a place that is better than this, Robin Ruff,
And I hope in my heart you'll go there;
Where the poor man's as great,
Though he hath no estate,
Ay, as though he'd a thousand a year, Robin Ruff,
As though he'd a thousand a year'"

"So you see," said Melody to the children, as they paced along, "it doesn't make any real difference whether we have things or don't have them. It's inside that one has to be happy; one can't be happy from the outside, ever. I should think it would be harder if one had lots of things that one must think about, and take care of, and perhaps worry over. I often am so glad I haven't many things."

They passed on, going down into the little meadow where the sweet rushes grew, for Melody knew that no child could stay cross when it had sweet rushes to play with; and Miss Vesta turned to the stranger with a quick, fierce movement. "Go away!" she cried. "You have your answer. Not for fifty thousand fortunes should you have the child! Go, and never come here again!"

* * * * *

It was two or three days after this that Dr. Brown was driving rapidly home toward the village. He had had a tiresome day, and he meant to have a cup of Vesta Dale's good tea and a song from Melody to smooth down his ruffled plumage, and to put him into good-humor again. His patients had been very trying, especially the last one he had visited,—an old lady who sent for him from ten miles' distance, and then told him she had taken seventy-five bottles of Vegetine without benefit, and wanted to know what she should do next. "I really do not know, Madam," the doctor replied, "unless you should pound up the seventy-five bottles with their labels, and take those." Whereupon he got into his buggy and drove off without another word.

But the Dale girls and Melody—bless them all for a set of angels!—would soon put him to rights again, thought the doctor, and he would send old Mrs. Prabbles some pills in the morning. There was nothing whatever the matter with the old harridan. Here was the turn; now in a moment he would see Vesta sitting in the doorway at her knitting, or looking out of Rejoice's window; and she would call the child whom his heart loved, and then for a happy, peaceful evening, and all vexations forgotten!

But what was this? Instead of the trim, staid figure he looked to see, who was this frantic woman who came running toward him from the little house, with white hair flying on the wind, with wild looks? Her dress was disordered; her eyes stared in anguish; her lips stammered, making confused sounds, which at first had no meaning to the startled hearer. But he heard—oh, he heard and understood, when the distracted woman grasped his arm, and cried,—

"Melody is stolen! stolen! and Rejoice is dead!"

CHAPTER VII.

LOST.

Miss Rejoice was not dead; though the doctor had a moment of dreadful fright when he saw her lying all crumpled up on the floor, her eyes closed, her face like wrinkled wax. Between them, the doctor and Miss Vesta got her back into bed, and rubbed her hands, and put stimulants between her closed lips. At last her breath began to flutter, and then came back steadily. She opened her eyes; at first they were soft and mild as usual, but presently a wild look stole into them.

"The child!" she whispered; "the child is gone!"

"We know it," said Dr. Brown, quietly. "We shall find her, Rejoice, never fear. Now you must rest a few minutes, and then you shall tell us how it happened. Why, we found you on the floor, my child,"—Miss Rejoice was older than the doctor, but it seemed natural to call her by any term of endearment,—"how upon earth did you get there?"

Slowly, with many pauses for breath and composure, Miss Rejoice told her story. It was short enough. Melody had been sitting with her, reading aloud from the great book which now lay face downward on the floor by the window. Milton's "Paradise Lost" it was, and Rejoice Dale could never bear to hear the book named in her life after this time. A carriage drove up and stopped at the door, and Melody went out to see who had come. As she went, she said, "It is a strange wagon; I have never heard it before." They both supposed it some stranger who had stopped to ask for a glass of water, as people often did, driving through the village on their way to the mountains. The sick woman heard a man speaking, in smooth, soft tones; she caught the words: "A little drive—fine afternoon;" and Melody's clear voice replying, "No, thank you, sir; you are very kind, but my aunt and I are alone, and I could not leave her. Shall I bring you a glass of water?" Then—oh, then— there was a sound of steps, a startled murmur in the beloved voice, and then a scream. Oh, such a scream! Rejoice Dale shrank down in her bed, and cried out herself in agony at the memory of it. She had called, she had shrieked aloud, the helpless creature, and her only answer was another cry of anguish: "Help! help! Auntie! Doctor! Rosin! Oh, Rosin, Rosin, help!" Then the cry was muffled, stifled, sank away into dreadful silence; the wagon drove off, and all was over. Rejoice Dale found herself on the floor, dragging herself along on her elbows. Paralyzed from the waist down, the body was a weary weight to drag, but she clutched at a chair, a table; gained a little way at each movement; thought she was nearly at the door, when sense and strength failed, and she knew nothing more till she saw her sister and the doctor bending over her.

Then Miss Vesta, very pale, with lips that trembled, and voice that would not obey her will, but broke and quavered, and failed at times, like a strange instrument one has not learned how to master,—Miss Vesta told her story, of the dark stranger who had come three days before and taken her up to a pinnacle, and showed her the kingdoms of the earth.

"I did not tell you, Rejoice," she cried, holding her sister's hand, and gazing into her face in an agony of self-reproach; "I did not tell you, because I was really tempted,—not for myself, I do believe; I am permitted to believe, and it is the one comfort I have,—but for you, Rejoice, my dear, and for the child herself. But mostly for you, oh, my God! mostly for you. And when I came to myself and knew you would rather die ten times over than have luxuries bought with the child's happy, innocent life,—when I came to myself, I was ashamed, and did not tell you, for I did not want you to think badly of me. If I had told you, you would have been on your guard, and have put me on mine; and I should never have left you, blind fool that I was, for you would have showed me the danger. Doctor, we are two weak women,—she in body, I in mind and heart. Tell us what we shall do, or I think we must both die!"

Dr. Brown hardly heard her appeal, so deeply was he thinking, wondering, casting about in his mind for counsel. But Rejoice Dale took her sister's hand in hers.

"'Though a thousand fall beside thee, and ten thousand at thy right hand, yet it shall not come nigh thee,'" she said steadfastly. "Our blind child is in her Father's hand, Sister; He leads her, and she can go nowhere without Him. Go you now, and seek for her."

"I cannot!" cried Vesta Dale, wringing her hands and weeping. "I cannot leave you, Rejoice. You know I cannot leave you."

Both women felt for the first time, with a pang unspeakable, the burden of restraint. The strong woman wrung her hands again, and moaned like a dumb creature in pain; the helpless body of the cripple quivered and shrank away from itself, but the soul within was firm.

"You must go," said Miss Rejoice, quietly. "Neither of us could bear it if you stayed. If I know you are searching, I can be patient; and I shall have help."

"Amanda Loomis could come," said Miss Vesta, misunderstanding her.

"Yes," said Rejoice, with a faint smile; "Amanda can come, and I shall do very well indeed till you come back with the child. Go at once, Vesta; don't lose a moment. Put on your bonnet and shawl, and Doctor will drive you over to the Corners. The stage goes by in an hour's time, and you have none too long to reach it."

Dr. Brown seemed to wake suddenly from the distressful dream in which he had been plunged. "Yes, I will drive you over to the stage, Vesta," he said. "God help me! it is all I can do. I have an operation to perform at noon. It is a case of life and death, and I have no right to leave it. The man's whole life is not worth one hour of Melody's," he added with some bitterness; "but that makes no difference, I suppose. I have no choice in the matter. Girls!" he cried, "you know well enough that if it were my own life, I would throw it down the well to give the child an hour's pleasure, let alone saving her from misery,—and perhaps from death!" he added to himself; for only he and the famous physician who had examined Melody at his instance knew that under all the joy and vigor of the child's simple, healthy life lay dormant a trouble of the heart, which would make any life of excitement or fatigue fatal to her in short space, though she might live in quiet many happy years. Yes, one other person knew this,—his friend Dr. Anthony, whose remonstrances against the wickedness of hiding this rare jewel from a world of appreciation and of fame could only be silenced by showing him the bitter drop which lay at the heart of the rose.

Rejoice Dale reassured him by a tender pressure of the hand, and a few soothing words. They had known each other ever since their pinafore days, these three people. He was younger than Miss Rejoice, and he had been deeply in love with her when he was an awkward boy of fifteen, and she a lovely seventeen-year-old girl. They had called him "doctor" at first in sport, when he came home to practise in his native village; but soon he had so fully shown his claim to the grave title that "the girls" and every one else had forgotten the fact that he had once been "Jack" to the whole village.

"Doctor," said the sick woman, "try not to think about it more than you can help! There are all the sick people looking to you as next to the hand of God; your path is clear before you."

Dr. Brown groaned. He wished his path were not so clear, that he might in some way make excuse to turn aside from it. "I will give Vesta a note to Dr. Anthony," he said, brightening a little at the thought. "He will do anything in his power to help us. There are other people, too, who will be kind. Yes, yes; we shall have plenty of help."

He fidgeted about the room, restless and uneasy, till Miss Vesta came in, in her bonnet and shawl. "I have no choice," he repeated doggedly, hugging his duty close, as if to dull the pressure of the pain within. "But how can you go alone, Vesta, my poor girl? You are not fit; you are trembling all over. God help us!" cried Dr. Brown, again.

For a moment the two strong ones stood irresolute, feeling themselves like little children in the grasp of a fate too big for them to grapple. The sick woman closed her eyes, and waited. God would help, in His good way. She knew no more, and no more was needed. There were a few moments of silence, as if all were waiting for something, they knew not what,—a sign, perhaps, that they were not forgotten, forsaken, on the sea of this great trouble.

Suddenly through the open window stole a breath of sound. Faint and far, it seemed at first only a note of the summer breeze, taking a deeper tone than its usual soft murmur. It deepened still; took form, rhythm; made itself a body of sound, sweet, piercing, thrilling on the ear. And at the sound of it, Vesta Dale fell away again into helpless weeping, like a frightened child; for it was the tune of "Rosin the Beau."

"Who shall tell him?" she moaned, covering her face with her hands, and rocking to and fro,—"oh, who shall tell him that the light of our life and his is gone out?"

CHAPTER VIII.

WAITING.

How did the time pass with the sick woman, waiting in the little chamber, listening day by day and hour by hour for the steps, the voices, which did not come? Miss Rejoice was very peaceful, very quiet,—too quiet, thought Mandy Loomis, the good neighbor who watched by her, fulfilling her little needs, and longing with a thirsty soul for a good dish of gossip. If Rejoice would only "open her mind!" it would be better for her, and such a relief to poor Mandy, unused to silent people who bore their troubles with a smile.

"Where do you s'pose she is, Rejoice?" Mrs. Loomis would cry, twenty times a day. "Where do you s'pose she is? Ef we only knew, 't would be easier to bear, seems 's though. Don't you think so, Rejoice?"

But Rejoice only shook her head, and said, "She is cared for, Mandy, we must believe. All we have to do is to be quiet, and wait for the Lord's time."

"Dear to goodness! She can wait!" exclaimed Mrs. Loomis to Mrs. Penny, when the latter came in one evening to see if any news had come. "She ain't done anything but wait, you may say, ever sence time was, Rejoice ain't. But I do find it dretful tryin' now, Mis' Penny, now I tell ye. Settin' here with my hands in my lap, and she so quiet in there, well, I do want to fly sometimes, seems 's though. Well, I am glad to see you, to be sure. The' ain't a soul ben by this day. Set down, do. You want to go in 'n' see Rejoice? Jest in a minute. I do think I shall have a sickness if I don't have some one to open my mind to. Now, Mis' Penny, where do you s'pose, where do you s'pose that child is?" Then, without waiting for a reply, she plunged headlong into the stream of talk.

"No, we ain't heard a word. Vesta went off a week ago, and Mr. De Arthenay with her. Providential, wasn't it, his happenin' along just in the nick o' time? I do get out of patience with Rejoice sometimes, takin' the Lord quite so much for granted as she doos; for, after all, the child was stole, you can't get over that, and seems's though if there'd ben such a good lookout as she thinks,—well, there! I don't want to be profane; but I will say 'twas a providence, Mr. De Arthenay happenin' along. Well, they went, and not a word have we heard sence but just one letter from Vesta, sayin' they hadn't found no trace yet, but they hoped to every day,—and land sakes, we knew that, I should hope. Dr. Brown comes in every day to cheer her up, though I do declare I need it more than she doos, seems's though. He's as close as an oyster, Dr. Brown is; I can't even get the news out of him, most times.

How's that boy of 'Bind Parker's,—him that fell and hurt his leg so bad? Gettin' well, is he?"

"No, he isn't," said Mrs. Penny, stepping in quickly on the question, as her first chance of getting in a word. "He's terrible slim; I heard Doctor say so. They're afraid of the kangaroo settin' in in the j'int, and you know that means death, sartin sure."

Both women nodded, drawing in their breath with an awful relish.

"'T will be a terrible loss to his mother," said Mandy Loomis. "Such a likely boy as he was gettin' to be, and 'Bind so little good, one way and another."

"Do you think they'll hear news of Melody?" asked Mrs. Penny, changing the subject abruptly.

Amanda Loomis plumped her hands down on her knees, and leaned forward; it was good to listen, but, oh, how much better it was to speak!

"I don't," she said, with gloomy emphasis. "If you ask me what I reelly think, Mis' Penny, it's that. I don't think we shall ever set eyes on that blessed child again. Rejoice is so sartin sure, sometimes my hopes get away with me, and I forgit my jedgment for a spell. But there! see how it is! Now, mind, what I say is for this room only." She spread her hands abroad, as if warning the air around to secrecy, and lowered her voice to an awestruck whisper. "I've ben here a week now, Mis' Penny. Every night the death-watch has ticked in Mel'dy's room the endurin' night. I don't sleep, you know, fit to support a flea. I hear every hour strike right straight along, and I know things that's hid from others, Mis' Penny, though I do say it. Last night as ever was I heard a sobbin' and a sighin' goin' round the house, as plain as I hear you this minute. Some might ha' said't was the wind, but there's other things besides wind, Mis' Penny; and I solemnly believe that was Mel'dy's sperrit, and the child is dead. It ain't my interest to say it," she cried, with a sudden change of tone, putting her apron to her eyes: "goodness knows it ain't my interest to say it. What that child has been to me nobody knows. When I've had them weakly spells, the' warn't nobody but Mel'dy could ha' brought me out of 'em alive, well I know. She tended me and sung to me like all the angels in heaven, and when she'd lay her hand on me—well, there! seems's though my narves 'ud quiet right down, and blow away like smoke. I've ben a well woman—that is to say, for one that's always enjoyed poor health—since Dr. Brown sent that blessed child to me. She has a gift, if ever any one had. Dr. Brown had ought to give her half of what he makes doctorin'; she's more help than all the medicine ever *he* gives. I never saw a doctor so dretful stingy with his stuff. Why, I've ben perishin' sometimes for want o' doctorin', and all he'd give me was a little pepsin, or tell me to take as much sody as would lay on the p'int of a penknife, or some such thing,—not so much as you'd give to a canary-bird. I do sometimes wish we had a doctor who knew the use o' medicine, 'stead of everlastin'ly talkin' about the laws o' health, and hulsome food, and all them notions. Why, there's old Dr. Jalap, over to the Corners. He give Beulah Pegrum seven Liver Pills at one dose, and only charged her fifty cents, over 'n' above the cost of the pills. Now *that's* what I call doctorin',—not but what I like Dr. Brown well enough. But Mel'dy—well, there! and now to have her took off so suddin, and never to know whether she's buried respectable, or buried at all! You hear awful stories of city ways, these times. Now, this is for this room only, and don't you ever tell a soul! It's as true as I live, they have a furnace where they burn folks' bodies, for all the world as if they was hick'ry lawgs. My cousin Salome's nephew that lives in the city saw one once. He thought it was connected with the gas-works, but he didn't know for sure. Mis' Penny, if Rejoice Dale was to know that Mel'dy was made into gas—"

Martha Penny clutched the speaker's arm, and laid her hand over her mouth, with a scared look. The door of the bedroom had swung open in the breeze, and in the stress of feeling Mandy Loomis had raised her voice higher and higher, till the last words rang through the house like the wail of a sibyl. But above the wail another sound was now rising, the voice of Rejoice Dale,— not calm and gentle, as they had always heard it, but high-pitched, quivering with intense feeling.

"I see her!" cried the sick woman. "I see the child! Lord, save her! Lord, save her!"

The two women hurried in, and found her sitting up in bed, her eyes wide, her arm outstretched, pointing—at what? Involuntarily they turned to follow the pointing finger, and saw the yellow-washed wall, and the wreath of autumn leaves that always hung there.

"What is it, Rejoice?" cried Mandy, terrified. "What do you see? Is it a spirit? Tell us, for pity's sake!"

But even at that moment a change came. The rigid muscles relaxed, the whole face softened to its usual peaceful look; the arm dropped gently, and Rejoice Dale sank back upon her pillow and smiled.

"Thy rod and thy staff!" she said. "Thy rod and thy staff! they comfort me." And for the first time since Melody was lost, she fell asleep, and slept like a little child.

CHAPTER IX.

BLONDEL.

Noontide in the great city! The July sun blazes down upon the brick sidewalks, heating them through and through, till they scorch the bare toes of the little street children, who creep about, sheltering their eyes with their hands, and keeping in the shade when it is possible. The apple-women crouch close to the wall, under their green umbrellas; the banana-sellers look yellow and wilted as their own wares. Men pass along, hurrying, because they are Americans, and business must go on whether it be hot or cold; but they move in a dogged jog-trot, expressive of weariness and disgust, and wipe their brows as they go, muttering anathemas under their breath on the whole summer season. Most of the men are in linen coats, some in no coats at all; all wear straw hats, and there is a great display of palm-leaf fans, waving in all degrees of energy. Here and there is seen an umbrella, but these are not frequent, for it seems to the American a strange and womanish thing to carry an umbrella except for rain; it also requires attention, and takes a man's mind off his business. Each man of all the hurrying thousands is shut up in himself, carrying his little world, which is all the world there is, about with him, seeing the other hurrying mites only "as trees walking," with no thought or note of them. Who cares about anybody else when it is so hot? Get through the day's work, and away to the wife and children in the cool by the sea-shore, or in the comfortable green suburb, where, if one must still be hot, one can at least suffer decently, and not "like a running river be,"—with apologies to the boy Chatterton.

Among all these hurrying motes in the broad, fierce stream of sunshine, one figure moves slowly, without haste. Nobody looks at anybody else, or this figure might attract some attention, even in the streets of the great city. An old man, tall and slender, with snowy hair falling in a single curl over his forehead; with brown eyes which glance birdlike here and there, seeing everything, taking in every face, every shadow of a vanishing form that hurries along and away from him; with fiddle-bow in hand, and fiddle held close and tenderly against his shoulder. De Arthenay, looking for his little girl!

Not content with scanning every face as it passes, he looks up at the houses, searching with eager eye their blank, close-shuttered walls, as if in hope of seeing through the barriers of brick and stone, and surprising the secrets that may lurk within. Now and then a house seems to take his fancy, for he stops, and still looking up at the windows, plays a tune. It is generally the same tune,—a simple, homely old air, which the street-boys can readily take up and whistle, though they do not hear it in the music-halls or on the hand-organs. A languid crowd gathers round him when he pauses thus, for street-boys know a good fiddler when they hear him; and this is a good fiddler.

When a crowd has collected, the old man turns his attention from the silent windows (they are generally silent; or if a face looks out, it is not the beloved one which is in his mind night and day, day and night) and scans the faces around him, with sad, eager eyes. Then, stopping short in his playing, he taps sharply on his fiddle, and asks in a clear voice if any one has seen or heard of a blind child, with beautiful brown hair, clear blue eyes, and the most wonderful voice in the world.

No one has heard of such a child; but one tells him of a blind negro who can play the trombone, and another knows of a blind woman who tells fortunes "equal to the best mejums;" and so on, and so on. He shakes his head with a patient look, makes his grand bow, and passes on to the next street, the next wondering crowd, the next disappointment. Sometimes he is hailed by some music-hall keeper who hears him play, and knows a good thing when he hears it, and who engages the old fiddler to play for an evening or two. He goes readily enough; for there is no knowing where the dark stranger may have taken the child, and where no clew is, one may follow any track that presents itself. So the old man goes, and sits patiently in the hot, noisy place. At first the merry-makers, who are not of a high degree of refinement, make fun of him, and cut many a joke at the expense of his blue coat and brass buttons, his nankeen trousers and old-fashioned stock. But he heeds them not; and once he begins to play, they forget all about his looks, and only want to dance, dance, and say there never was such music for dancing. When a pleasant-looking girl comes near him, or pauses in the dance, he calls her to him, and asks her in a low tone the usual question: has she seen or heard of a blind child, with the most beautiful hair, etc. He is careful whom he asks, however; he would not insult Melody by asking for her of some of these young women, with bold eyes, with loose hair and disordered looks. So he sits and plays, a quaint, old-world figure, among the laughing, dancing, foolish crowd. Old De Arthenay, from the Androscoggin,—what would his ancestor, the gallant Marquis who came over with Baron Castine to America, what would the whole line of ancestors, from the crusaders down, say to see their descendant in such a place as this? He has always held his head high, though he has earned his bread by fiddling, varied by shoemaking in the winter-time. He has always kept good company, he would tell you, and would rather go hungry any day than earn a dinner among people who do not regard the decencies of life. Even in this place, people come to feel the quality of the old man, somehow, and no one speaks rudely to him; and voices are even lowered as they pass him, sitting grave and erect on his stool, his magic bow flying, his foot keeping time to the music. All the old tunes he plays, "Money

Musk," and "Portland Fancy," and "Lady of the Lake." Now he quavers into the "Chorus Jig;" but no one here knows enough to dance that, so he comes back to the simpler airs again. And as he plays, the whole tawdry, glaring scene drops away from the old man's eyes, and instead of vulgar gaslight he sees the soft glow of the afternoon sun on the country road, and the graceful elms bending in an arch overhead, as if to watch the child Melody as she dances. The slender figure swaying hither and thither, with its gentle, wind-blown motion, the exquisite face alight with happiness, the floating tendrils of hair, the most beautiful hair in the world; then the dear, homely country folks sitting by the roadside, watching with breathless interest his darling, their darling, the flower of the whole country-side; Miss Vesta's tall, stately figure in the doorway; the vine-clad window, behind which Rejoice lies, unseen, yet sharing all the sweet, simple pleasure with heartfelt enjoyment,— all this the old fiddler sees, set plain before him. The "lady" on his arm (for De Arthenay's fiddle is a lady as surely as he is a gentleman),—the lady feels it too, perhaps, for she thrills to his touch, as the bow goes leaping over the strings; and more than one wild girl and rough fellow feels a touch of something that has not been felt mayhap for many a day, and goes home to stuffy garret or squalid cellar the better for that night's music. And when it is over, De Arthenay makes his stately bow once more, and walks round the room, asking his question in low tones of such as seem worthy of it; and then home, patient, undaunted, to the quiet lodging where Vesta Dale is sitting up for him, weary after her day's search in other quarters of the city, hoping little from his coming, yet unwilling to lie down without a sight of his face, always cheery when it meets hers, and the sound of his voice saying,—

"Better luck to-morrow, Miss Vesta! better luck tomorrow! There's One has her in charge, and He didn't need us to-day; that's all, my dear."

God help thee, De Arthenay! God speed and prosper thee, Rosin the Beau!

But is not another name more fitting even than the fantastic one of his adoption? Is not this Blondel, faithful, patient, undaunted, wandering by tower and town, singing his song of love and hope and undying loyalty under every window, till it shall one day fall like a breath from heaven on the ear of the prisoner, sitting in darkness and the shadow of death?

CHAPTER X.

DARKNESS.

"And how's our sweet little lady to-day? She's looking as pretty as a picture, so it's a pleasure to look at her. How are you feeling, dearie?"

It was a woman's voice that spoke, soft and wheedling, yet with a certain unpleasant twang in it. She spoke to Melody, who sat still, with folded hands, and head bowed as if in a dream.

"I am well, thank you," answered the child; and she was silent again.

The woman glanced over her shoulder at a man who had followed her into the room,—a dark man with an eager face and restless, discontented eyes; the same man who had watched Melody over the wall of the old burying-ground, and heard her sing. He had never heard her sing since, save for that little snatch of "Robin Ruff," which she had sung to the children the day when he stood and pleaded with Vesta Dale to sell her soul for her sister's comfort.

"And here's Mr. Anderson come to see you, according to custom," said the woman; "and I hope you are glad to see him, I'm sure, for he's your best friend, dearie, and he does love you so; it would be quite surprising, if you weren't the sweet lamb you are, sitting there like a flower all in the dark."

She paused, and waited for a reply; but none came. The two exchanged a glance of exasperation, and the woman shook her fist at the child; but her voice was still soft and smooth as she resumed her speech.

"And you'll sing us a little song now, dearie, won't you? To think that you've been here near a week now, and I haven't heard the sound of that wonderful voice yet, only in speaking. It's sweet as an angel's then, to be sure; but dear me! if you knew what Mr. Anderson has told me about his hearing you sing that day! Such a particular gentleman as he is, too, anybody would tell you! Why, I've seen girls with voices as they thought the wonder of the world, and their friends with them, and Mr. Anderson would no more listen to them than the dirt under his feet; no, indeed, he wouldn't. And you that he thinks so much of! why, it makes me feel real bad to see you not take that comfort in him as you might. Why, he wants to be a father to you, dearie. He hasn't got any little girl of his own, and he will give you everything that's nice, that he will, just as soon as you begin to get a little fond of him, and realize all he's doing for you. Why, most young ladies would give their two eyes for your chance, I can tell you."

She was growing angry in spite of herself, and the man Anderson pulled her aside.

"It's no use," he said. "We shall just have to wait. You know, my dear," he continued, addressing the child, "you know that you will never see your aunts again unless you *do* sing. You sense that, do you?"

No reply. Melody shivered a little, then drew herself together and was still,— the stillest figure that ever breathed and lived. Anderson clenched his hands and fairly trembled with rage and with the effort to conceal it. He must not frighten the child too much. He could not punish her, hurt her in any way; for any shock might injure the precious voice which was to make his fortune. He was no fool, this man. He had some knowledge, more ambition. He had been unsuccessful on the whole, had been disappointed in several ventures; now he had found a treasure, a veritable gold-mine, and-he could not work it! Could anything be more exasperating? This child, whose voice could rouse a whole city—a city! could rouse the world to rapture, absolutely refused to sing a note! He had tried cajolery, pathos, threats; he had called together a chosen company of critics to hear the future Catalani, and had been forced to send them home empty, having heard no note of the marvellous voice! The child would not sing, she would not even speak, save in the briefest possible fashion, little beyond "yes" and "no."

What was a poor impresario to do? He longed to grasp her by the shoulders and shake the voice out of her; his hands fairly itched to get hold of the obstinate little piece of humanity, who, in her childishness, her helplessness, her blindness, thus defied him, and set all his cherished plans at nought.

And yet he would not have shaken her probably, even had he dared to do so. He was not a violent man, nor a wholly bad one. He could steal a child, and convince himself that it was for the child's good as well as his own; but he could not hurt a child. He had once had a little girl of his own; it was quite true that he had intended to play a father's part to Melody, if she would only have behaved herself. In the grand drama of success that he had arranged so carefully, it was a most charming role that he had laid out for himself. Anderson the benefactor, Anderson the discoverer, the adopted father of the prodigy, the patron of music. Crowds hailing him with rapturous gratitude; the wonder-child kneeling and presenting him with a laurel crown, which had been thrown to her, but which she rightly felt to be his due, who had given her all, and brought her from darkness into light! Instead of this, what part was this he was really playing? Anderson the kidnapper; Anderson the villain, the ruffian, the invader of peaceful homes, the bogy to scare naughty children with. He did not say all this to himself, perhaps, because he was not, save when carried away by professional enthusiasm, an imaginative man; but he felt thoroughly uncomfortable, and, above all, absolutely at sea, not knowing which way to turn. As he stood thus, irresolute, the woman by his side eying him furtively from time to time, Melody turned her face toward him and spoke.

"If you will take me home," she said, "I will sing to you. I will sing all day, if you like. But here I will never sing. It would not be possible for you to make me do it, so why do you try? You made a mistake, that is all."

"Oh, that's all, is it?" repeated Anderson.

"Yes, truly," the child went on. "Perhaps you do not mean to be unkind,—Mrs. Brown says you do not; but then why *are* you unkind, and why will you not take me home?"

"It is for your own good, child," repeated Anderson, doggedly. "You know that well enough. I have told you how it will all be, a hundred times. You were not meant for a little village, and a few dull old people; you are for the world, the great world of wealth and fashion and power. If you were not either a fool or—or—I don't know what, you would see the matter as it really is. Mrs. Brown is right: most girls would give their eyes, and their ears too, for such a chance as you have. You are only a child, and a very foolish child; and you don't know what is good for you. Some day you will be thankful to me for making you sing."

Melody smiled, and her smile said much, for Anderson turned red, and clenched his hands fiercely.

"You belong to the world, I tell you!" he cried again. "The world has a right to you."

"To the world?" the child repeated softly. "Yes, it is true; I do belong to the world,—to God's world of beauty, to the woods and fields, the flowers and grasses, and to the people who love me. When the birds sing to me I can answer them, and they know that my song is as sweet as their own. The brook tells me its story, and I tell it again, and every ripple sounds in my voice; and I know that I please the brook, and all who hear me,—little beasts, and flowers that nod on their stems to hear, and trees that bend down to touch me, and tell me by their touch that they are well pleased. And children love to hear me sing, and I can fill their little hearts with joy. I sing to sick people, and they are easier of their pain, and perhaps they may sleep, when they have not been able to sleep for long nights. This is my life, my work. I am God's child; and do you think I do not know the work my Father has given me to do?" With a sudden movement she stepped forward, and laid her hand lightly on the man's breast. "You are God's child, too!" she said, in a low voice. "Are you doing His work now?"

There was silence in the room. Anderson was as if spellbound, his eyes fixed on the child, who stood like a youthful prophetess, her head thrown back, her beautiful face full of solemn light, her arm raised in awful appeal. The woman threw her apron over her head and began to cry. The man moistened his lips twice or thrice, trying to speak, but no words came. At length he made a sign of despair to his accomplice; moved back from that questioning, warning hand, whose light touch seemed to burn through and through him,—moved away, groping for the door, his eyes still fixed on the child's face; stole out finally, as a thief steals, and closed the door softly behind him.

Melody stood still, looking up to heaven. A great peace filled her heart, which had been so torn and tortured these many days past, ever since the dreadful moment when she had been forced away from her home, from her life, and brought into bondage and the shadow of death. She had thought till to-day that she should die. Not that she was deserted, not that God had forgotten,—oh, no; but that He did not need her any longer here, that she had not been worthy of the work she had thought to be hers, and that now she was to be taken elsewhere to some other task. She was only a child; her life was strong in every limb; but God could not mean her to live here, in this way,—that would not be merciful, and His property was always to have mercy. So death would come,—death as a friend, just as Auntie Joy had always described him; and she would go hence, led by her Father's hand.

But now, what change was coming over her? The air seemed lighter, clearer, since Anderson had left the room. A new hope entered her heart, coming she knew not whence, filling it with pulses and waves of joy. She thought of her home; and it seemed to grow nearer, more distinct, at every moment. She saw (as blind people see) the face of Rejoice Dale, beaming with joy and peace; she felt the strong clasp of Miss Vesta's hand. She smelt the lilacs, the white lilacs beneath which she loved to sit and sing. She heard—oh, God! what did she hear? What sound was this in her ears? Was it still the dream, the lovely dream of home, or was a real sound thrilling in her ears, beating in her heart, filling the whole world with the voice of hope,—of hope fulfilled, of life and love?

> "I've travelled this country all over,
> And now to the next I must go;
> But I know that good quarters await me,
> And a welcome to Rosin the Beau."

Oh, Father of mercy! never doubted, always near in sorrow and in joy! oh, holy angels, who have held my hands and lifted me up, lest I dash my foot against a stone! A welcome,—oh, on my knees, in humble thanksgiving, in endless love and praise,—a welcome to Rosin the Beau!

* * * * *

An hour later Mrs. Brown stood before her employer, flushed and disordered, making her defence.

"I couldn't have helped it, not if I had died for it, Mr. Anderson. You couldn't have helped it yourself, if you had been there. When she heard that fiddle, the child dropped on her knees as if she had been shot, and I thought she was going to faint. But the next minute she was at the window, and such a cry as she gave! the sound of it is in my bones yet, and will be till I die."

She paused, and wiped her fiery face, for she had run bareheaded through the blazing streets.

"Then he came in,—the old man. He was plain dressed, but he came in like a king to his throne; and the child drifted into his arms like a flake of snow, and there she lay. Mr. Anderson, when he held her there on his breast, and turned and looked at me, with his eyes like two black coals, all power was taken from me, and I couldn't have moved if it had been to save my own life. He pointed at me with his fiddle-bow, but it might have been a sword for all the difference I knew; anyway, his voice went through and through me like something sharp and bright. 'You cannot move,' he said; 'you have no power to move hand or foot till I have taken my child away. I bid you be still!' Mr. Anderson, sir, I *had* no power! I stood still, and they went away. They seemed to melt away together,—he with his arm round her waist, holding her up like; and she with her face turned up to his, and a look like heaven, if I ever hope to see heaven. The next minute they was gone, and still I hadn't never moved. And now I've come to tell you, sir," cried Mrs. Brown, smoothing down her ruffled hair in great agitation; "and to tell you something else too, as I would burst if I didn't. I am glad he has got her! If I was to lose my place fifty times over, as you've always been good pay and a kind gentleman too, still I say it, I'm glad he has got her. She wasn't of your kind, sir, nor of mine neither. And—and I've never been a professor," cried the woman, with her apron at her eyes, "but I hope I know an angel when I see one, and I mean to be a better woman from this day, so I do. And she asked God to bless me, Mr. Anderson, she did, as she went away, because I meant to be kind to her; and I did mean it, the blessed creature! And she said good-by to you too, sir; and she knew you thought it was for her good, only you didn't know what God meant. And I'm so glad, I'm so glad!"

She stopped short, more surprised than she had ever been in her life; for Edward Anderson was shaking her hand violently, and telling her that she was a good woman, a very good woman indeed, and that he thought the better of her, and had been thinking for some time of raising her salary.

CHAPTER XI.

LIGHT.

I love the morning light,—the freshness, the pearls and diamonds, the fairy linen spread on the grass to bleach (there be those who call it spider-web, but to such I speak not), the silver fog curling up from river and valley. I love it so much that I am loath to confess that sometimes the evening light is even more beautiful. Yet is there a softness that comes with the close of day, a glorification of common things, a drawing of purple shadows over all that is rough or unsightly, which makes the early evening perhaps the most perfect time of all the perfect hours.

It was such an hour that now brooded over the little village, when the people came out from their houses to watch for Melody's coming. It is a pretty little village at all times, very small and straggling, but lovely with flowers and vines and dear, homely old houses, which have not found out that they are again in the fashion out of which they were driven many years ago, but still hold themselves humbly, with a respect for the brick and stucco of which they have heard from time to time. It is always pretty, I say, but this evening it had received some fresh baptism of beauty, as if the Day knew what was coming, and had pranked herself in her very best for the festival. The sunbeams slanted down the straggling, grass-grown road, and straightway it became an avenue of wonder, with gold-dust under foot, flecked here and there with emerald. The elms met over head in triumphal arches; the creepers on the low houses hung out wonderful scarfs and banners of welcome, which swung gold and purple in the joyous light. And as the people came out of their houses, now that the time was drawing near, lo! the light was on their faces too; and the plain New England men and women, in their prints and jeans, shone like the figures in a Venetian picture, and were all a-glitter with gold and precious stones for once in their lives, though they knew it not.

But not all of this light came from the setting sun; on every face was the glow of a great joy, and every voice was soft with happiness, and the laughter was all a-tremble with the tears that were so near it. They were talking about the child who was coming back to them, whom they had mourned as lost. They were telling of her gracious words and ways, so different from anything else they had known,—her smiles, and the way she held her head when she sang; and the way she found things out, without ever any one telling her. Wonderful, was it not? Why, one dared not have ugly thoughts in her presence; or if they came, one tried to hide them away, deep down, so that Melody should not see them with her blind eyes. Do you remember how Joel Pottle took too much one day (nobody knows to this day where he got it, and his folks all temperance people), and how he stood out in the road and swore at the folks coming out of meeting, and how Melody came along and took him by the hand, and led him away down by the brook, and never left him till he was a sober man again? And every one knew Joel had never touched a drop of liquor from that day on.

Again, could they ever forget how she saved the baby,—Jane Pegrum's baby,—that had been forgotten by its frantic mother in the burning house? They shuddered as they recalled the scene: the writhing, hissing flames, the charred rafters threatening every moment to fall; and the blind child walking calmly along the one safe beam, unmoved above the pit of fire which none of them could bear to look on, catching the baby from its cradle ("and it all of a smoulder, just ready to burst out in another minute") and bringing it safe to the woman who lay fainting on the grass below! Vesta had never forgiven them for that, for letting the child go: she was away at the time, and when she came back and found Melody's eyebrows all singed off, it did seem as though the village wouldn't hold her, didn't it? And Doctor was just as bad. But, there! they couldn't have held her back, once she knew the child was there; and Rejoice was purely thankful. Melody seemed to favor Rejoice, almost as if she might be her own child. Vesta had more of this world in her, sure enough.

Isn't it about time for them to be coming? Doctor won't waste time on the road, you may be sure. Dreadful crusty he was this morning, if any one tried to speak to him. Miss Meechin came along just as he was harnessing up, and asked if he couldn't give her something to ease up her sciatica a little mite, and what do you think he said? "Take it to the Guinea Coast and drown it!" Not another word could she get out of him. Now, that's no way to talk to a patient. But Doctor hasn't been himself since Melody was stole; anybody could see that with his mouth. Look at how he's treated that man with the operation, that kept him from going to find the child himself! He never said a word to him, they say, and tended him as careful as a woman, every day since he got hurt; but just as soon as he got through with him, he'd go out in the yard, they say, and swear at the pump, till it would turn your blood cold to hear him. It's gospel truth, for I had it from the nurse, and she said it chilled her marrow. Yes, a violent man, Doctor always was; and, too, he was dreadful put out at the way the man got hurt,—reaching out of his buggy to slat his neighbor's cow, just because he had a spite against him. Seemed trifling, some thought, but he's like to pay for it. Did you hear the sound of wheels?

Look at Alice and Alfred, over there with the baby; bound to have the first sight of them, aren't they, standing on the wall like that? They are as happy as two birds, ever since they made up that time. Yes, Melody's doing too, that was. She didn't know it; but she doesn't know the tenth of what she does.

Just the sight of her coming along the road—hark! surely I heard the click of the doctor's mare. Does seem hard to wait, doesn't it? But Rejoice,—what do you suppose it is for Rejoice? only she's used to it, as you may say.

Yes, Rejoice is used to waiting, surely; what else is her life? In the little white cottage now, Mandy Loomis, in a fever of excitement, is running from door to window, flapping out flies with her apron, opening the oven door, fidgeting here and there like a distracted creature; but in the quiet room, where Rejoice lies with folded hands, all is peace, brooding peace and calm and blessedness. The sick woman does not even turn her head on the pillow; you would think she slept, if she did not now and again raise the soft brown eyes,—the most patient eyes in the world,—and turn them toward the window. Yes, Rejoice is used to waiting; yet it is she who first catches the far-off sound of wheels, the faint click of the brown mare's hoofs. With her bodily ears she hears it, though so still is she one might think the poor withered body deserted, and the joyous soul away on the road, hovering round the returning travellers as they make their triumphal entry.

For all can see them now. First the brown mare's head, with sharp ears pricked, coming round the bend; then a gleam of white, a vision of waving hair, a light form bending forward. Melody! Melody has come back to us! They shout and laugh and cry, these quiet people. Alfred and Alice his wife have run forward, and are caressing the brown mare with tears of joy, holding the baby up for Melody to feel and kiss, because it has grown so wonderfully in this week of her absence. Mrs. Penny is weeping down behind the hedge; Mandy Loomis is hurling herself out of the window as if bent on suicide; Dr. Brown pishes and pshaws, and blows his nose, and says they are a pack of ridiculous noodles, and he must give them a dose of salts all round to-morrow, as sure as his name is John Brown. On the seat behind him sits Melody, with Miss Vesta and the old fiddler on either side, holding a hand of each. She has hardly dared yet to loose her hold on these faithful hands; all the way from the city she has held them, with almost convulsive pressure. Very high De Arthenay holds his head, be sure! No marquis of all the line ever was prouder than he is this day. He kisses the child's little hand when he hears the people shout, and then shakes his snowy curl, and looks about him like a king. Vesta Dale has lost something of her stately carriage. Her face is softer than people remember it, and one sees for the first time a resemblance to her sister. And Dr. Brown—oh, he fumes and storms at the people, and calls them a pack of noodles; but for all that, he cannot drive ten paces without turning round to make sure that it is all true,—that here is Melody on the back seat, come home again, home, never to leave them again.

But, hush, hush, dear children, running beside the wagon with cries of joy and happy laughter! Quiet, all voices of welcome, ringing out from every throat, making the little street echo from end to end! Quiet all, for Melody is singing! Standing up, held fast by those faithful hands on either side, the child lifts her face to heaven, lifts her heart to God, lifts up her voice in the evening hymn,—

"Jubilate, jubilate!
Jubilate, amen!"

The people stand with bowed heads, with hands folded as if in prayer. What is prayer, if this be not it? The evening light streams down, warm, airy gold; the clouds press near in pomp of crimson and purple. The sick woman holds her peace, and sees the angels of God ascending and descending, ministering to her. Put off thy shoes from thy feet, for the place whereon thou standest is holy ground.

"Jubilate, jubilate!
Jubilate, amen!"

THE END.

Buy Books Online from

www.Booksophile.com

Explore our collection of books written in various languages and uncommon topics from different parts of the world, including history, art and culture, poems, autobiography and bibliographies, cooking, action & adventure, world war, fiction, science, and law.

Add to your bookshelf or gift to another lover of books - first editions of some of the most celebrated books ever published. From classic literature to bestsellers, you will find many first editions that were presumed to be out-of-print.

Free shipping globally for orders worth US$ 100.00.

Use code "Shop_10" to avail additional 10% on first order.

Visit today
www.booksophile.com